GIDEON'S DAY

This is the story of one man's day at Scotland Yard. In the course of this one long day, Detective-Superintendent George Gideon has almost every type of crime to deal with, from murder to mail-van robbery. This new kind of thriller gives a vivid picture of the "policeman's lot".

J. J. MARRIC

GIDEON'S DAY

London
HODDER & STOUGHTON

FIRST PRINTED - 1955

Made and Printed in Great Britain
for Hodder and Stoughton Limited
by Ebenezer Baylis and Son Limited
The Trinity Press, Worcester and
London

CONTENTS

CHAPTER ONE

GIDEON'S WRATH

THE wrath of Gideon was remarkable to see and a majestic thing to hear. Among other things, it transformed Gideon himself. From a massive, slow-moving, pale man with a quiet voice and unassuming, almost modest manner, he became as a raging lion, cheeks reddening and voice bellowing. Such times did not come often; but as Gideon was a superintendent at New Scotland Yard, whenever it did, it made many people uneasy, and set them searching their consciences for evidence of things undone or badly done. All the sins of omission and commission noticed by Gideon but not used in evidence against his subordinates, became vivid in the recollection of the offenders; on any one of these, Gideon might descend. The first cause of the storm often suffered lightly compared with others. One consequence was inescapable; a shaking up. The thin, chill, sardonic reproof of the Assistant Commissioner, the curt disapproval of the Secretary, even the cold or hot wind created by the induction of a new Commissioner, were petty trials compared with the wrath of Gideon, for he was the Yard's senior superintendent, and regarded by many as its Grand Old Man.

Yet Gideon was not yet fifty.

On the occasion under discussion the first signs of the wrath to come were visible when Gideon drove too fast into the approaches to the Yard, swinging his new-looking black Wolseley off the Embankment at Flying Squad pace. He squeezed between the A.C.'s Daimler and Mr. Millington's Riley at fully twenty-five miles an hour and had only a foot to spare on one side and six inches on the other. He brought the car to a standstill with its bumper a bare inch off the wall, more by luck than judgment.

Quite evidently, this was going to be Gideon's day.

Five officers, all uniformed, read the signs.

By the time Gideon reached the foot of the stone steps leading to the main hall of the C.I.D. building, the news, in the form of a "get everything under control, G.G.'s on the warpath" warning, was on its way through the Yard, via a one-armed lift attendant, two plainclothes sergeants and a telephone operator named Veronica (who was engaged to one of the sergeants). It quivered along telephone lines, cut into large offices and small like a draught of cold wind; it reached the canteen, the divers departments from the laboratory to ballistics, and made the men on radio-control duty much brisker in the Information Room. In fact, by the time Gideon reached his own office, it had reached the ears of the Secretary, that almost anonymous personage who knew practically everything that went on.

The Secretary grinned.

Few others found it even slightly amusing, for even at the Yard a completely clear conscience is a rarity. Chief Inspector Lemaitre, who shared Gideon's office, had two minutes' notice of the storm. That was time in which to straighten his tie, put on his coat, empty the seven cigarette stubs out of his ashtray and then, for appearances' sake, pick up two and put them back. He also had time to stack the morning's reports on Gideon's desk, under three headings: *New Inquiries*, *Inquiries Proceeding*, and *Investigation Closed*. That done, he trundled back to his own desk, lifted the telephone and called 1B Division; he considered it wise to be on the telephone, for that would give him time to judge the likely effect of the tempest on him. Lemaitre was just a year younger than Gideon, a thin, lanky and laconic man, showing to all except Gideon a confidence which suggested that he was sure that he could never be wrong. In fact, he was prone to the mistakes which usually follow over-confidence.

He was holding on for the call when the door opened, banged back against the doorstop, and admitted Gideon. It was rather as if an elephant had changed its slow, stately progress for the furious speed of a gazelle; except that Gideon was not even remotely like a gazelle.

He looked round at Lemaitre, who raised a hand and gave

a bright smile; and allowed it to freeze on his lantern cheeks, as if he had received no warning.

Gideon pushed the chair behind his own desk into position, so that it banged against the wall. He dropped into it, and stretched out for the telephone. He looked across at Lemaitre, his big, grey eyebrows thrust forward, his lined forehead narrowed in a scowl, hooked nose quivering slightly at the nostrils, as if under the influence of an unfamiliar smell. In his big way, Gideon was distinguished-looking, with his iron-grey hair, that nose, arched lips, a big, square chin. His looks would have been an asset in almost any profession from the law to politics, and especially in the Church; as a detective, they occasionally helped to impress a jury, especially when there were several women on it.

"Give me Foster," he said into the telephone.

Lemaitre thought of a youngish, up-and-coming detective, spruce-looking, but unpopular. What had Foster done to cause such a storm as this? Lemaitre speculated hopefully; then his call came through but the man he wanted wasn't in. That was an advantage after all.

"I'll call him later," he said, and rang off. He smiled brightly. "Morning, George."

Gideon nodded and grunted, but obviously was thinking of the telephone. A faint murmur came from it, and Gideon said:

"Come and see me, Foster, at once."

He put down the receiver so heavily that the bell sounded. Then he placed both hands on his desk, fingers spread, and kept them very still as he looked at Lemaitre. The Chief Inspector probably had more experience of Gideon's wrath than anyone else at the Yard, and was quite sure that the cause of this was really serious. Gideon seldom if ever let himself go so utterly unless he had been given grim cause.

"What's up, George?" Lemaitre asked.

"Blurry fool," Gideon said. "Blurry crook, if it comes to that. I haven't felt as vicious as this for years. You get out, Lem, tell you about it afterwards. Get out as soon as he comes in."

"Okay," promised Lemaitre.

There was room for nothing else on Gideon's mind, another ominous sign; and when he talked of a C.I.D. man as a crook, it was more than ominous, it was alarming. Lemaitre felt uneasy for a deeper reason now.

The "blurry" instead of "bloody" meant nothing. When these two men had first met, nearly twenty-five years ago, Gideon had commanded the vocabulary of a trooper who had served his apprenticeship in Covent Garden market. He had always known exactly when to use it, and had first started toning it down precisely twenty years ago this spring.

He'd been a detective-sergeant then, with the same promise as young Foster. "Blurry" had been his first substitution, uttered to Lemaitre's open-mouthed astonishment. Lemaitre, then also a detective-sergeant, hadn't been even slightly nervous of Gideon, although he had willingly conceded him best in most aspects of detective work.

"What's got into you?" he had asked. "Toothache?"

"Toothache be *blowed*," Gideon had said, and grinned fiercely. "Sent young Tom to Sunday School yesterday for the first time, when he came back Kate and I asked him how he liked it. Know what he said? 'Bloody good,' he said, so we weighed into him about wicked words, and know what he said then? He said it was what *I'd* said after seeing a film the night before. I had, too. From now on, I've got to mind my language if I don't want trouble with Kate. The kid's too young to start, anyway."

Lemaitre hadn't heard Gideon swear for many years.

He'd had good enough reason for watching his language, of course; young Tom had been the first of six and the youngest child was only eight now. Or was it ten? Lemaitre was not quite sure.

There was a tap at the door. "Come in," Gideon called, and the door opened and Foster came in smartly. He dressed well, was tall, well-built, and had quite a name in amateur rugby and tennis circles. Aged about thirty, Lemaitre thought, and if he didn't think himself so clever and stopped putting on airs, he would be rated high.

Lemaitre stood up.

"Just going along to Records," he said, "won't be long."

Gideon grunted.

Foster said: "Good morning, sir," in just about the right tone and manner. He did not look puzzled, apprehensive or guilty. Lemaitre even wondered whether the whisper of the wrath had reached him, he looked almost too bland for that. His dark hair was brushed flat down and straight back from his forehead; his rather bold eyes and nose told the discerning that he would be too interested in Number One. Lemaitre went out, reluctantly, and subdued the temptation to stand at the door and listen. He strolled off towards the canteen for a cup of tea, calling on Records *en route* in case Gideon telephoned him there. They would say that he'd been and gone. The fact that Lemaitre thought that a necessary precaution was an indication of the awe he felt at times for Gideon.

In the office, the detective-sergeant looked down at the Superintendent.

Gideon's hands were still on the desk, palms downwards, skin a leathery-looking brown, fingers and nails big and strong but not at all ugly. The cuffs of a clean white shirt showed. He wore a suit of navy blue and a blue and white spotted tie, all of good quality.

His eyes were slatey blue, big, with heavy, sleepy-looking lids—but there was nothing sleepy about them now. He was a man burning with anger. Foster, at first completely at ease, began to look less self-confident. That became worse because he had to stand in front of the desk like a schoolboy before an unpredictable master; after a few seconds he actually moistened his lips and broke the harsh silence.

"You—you sent for me, sir?"

"Yes," Gideon said, very heavily. "I sent for you, Foster. I sent for you to tell you a thing or two." His voice was deep and rather husky; just now he gave the impression that he was trying not to raise it. "I sent for you to tell you that you're a living disgrace to the C.I.D. and the Metropolitan Police Force generally. In all my years on the Force I've met some fools and a few knaves and here and there a rat, and you're one of the big rats. I ought to put you on a charge right away and make sure it sticks, and I'm not sure that I won't. We make mistakes here at the Yard, and occasionally let a rogue in, but you're the first of your kind I've come across, and I'd like to break your neck."

All Foster's blandness had vanished. His thick, full lips were red and wet, where he kept locking them. His cheeks had no colour left, and his almost black eyes couldn't keep steady. When Gideon stopped talking, Foster gulped, tried to find words, but couldn't. Gideon sat there, motionless, damning, as if challenging him to say a word in his defence.

Foster gulped again and eased his collar.

"I—I think you ought to be—to be very careful about talking that way," he said thinly. "You've no right to——"

"I've sent Chief Inspector Lemaitre out of the office," Gideon cut across the protest abruptly, "so we can have this interview between ourselves, without witnesses. But I can get all the witnesses I want to prove that you're a skunk. Only skunk isn't the best word. You're a renegade and you're a traitor, and if you were in the army you'd be shot and I'd be glad to pull the trigger."

Now Foster went red.

"Who the hell do you think you're talking to?"

"At the moment to Detective-Sergeant Eric Foster, of the Criminal Investigation Department," Gideon growled, "but you won't be able to call yourself that for long."

Foster still tried bluster.

"What's this all about? What are you accusing me of doing?"

"If you want it in simple words, I'm accusing you, as an officer of the Criminal Investigation Department, of accepting bribes and so deliberately failing to carry out your duty. I know who's been paying you and I know why, and I've a pretty good idea how much money you've had over the past three months. Like to know how I know?" The big hands didn't move, the gaze of the slatey-blue eyes didn't falter. "Because an *honest* crook told me. He said that he didn't mind cracking a crib or doing a smash-and-grab job, but when it came to feeding dope to kids in their teens, he drew a line—and he thought I ought to, too."

Foster exclaimed: "He's lying! There was no dope——"

He broke off, and all his colour died away, leaving only his shiny dark eyes.

Gideon said heavily: "That's right, say that you didn't know that they were selling reefers, or that one of them had a hypo and was selling shots of the muck for a guinea a time. Say you thought it was just a question of selling intoxicating liquor after hours—how much better policeman are you for that? You've got a job to do, and if you'd kept your eyes open you would have known what was going on. Even I can't believe that you knew about the dope. You——"

"Of course I didn't," Foster put in quickly. "I—I didn't know about selling drink after hours, either."

Gideon shook his head, slowly, deliberately, massively.

"Foster," he said, "you haven't even the sense not to lie about it. I suppose you've got to lie. It's the only way you might be able to save your skin. So you'll try." Much of the power had gone from Gideon's voice, as if what had happened had exhausted him. "And Chang will lie, too, because if he admitted it, he knows his club would be closed up and he wouldn't be allowed to open up again in London. I don't doubt that you're paid off in a dark corner, that no one sees you meet and no one else knows anything about it—or so you think. Or you *thought*." The sneer was devastating. "Well, now you know better. Now you know you can't get away with accepting bribes. From this day on, you'll know what it's like to realize that thanks to you, some kids have become cocaine addicts, and that it's ruined their whole lives."

Foster said between clenched teeth: "If kids want dope they'll find a way of getting it. And whoever told you that I've been taking bribes is a liar. You say you got a squeak—I want to know who from." He paused. "I know the kind who squeal about things like that. I know the kind who squeal to *you*, too." Foster's sneer rivalled Gideon's; in fact, it was uglier. "Old lags, blackguards who ought to be inside and would be if you did your job properly, but you let them keep out, so that you can get them to squeal on others. Think I don't know? Think I don't know that the name of Gideon stinks in the West End?"

When he stopped, it was almost fearfully, as if suddenly

afraid that he had gone too far. But Gideon did not move; just looked at him as he might at something unclean. Foster ran his tongue along his lips.

"I—I'm sorry, sir, I didn't mean that. It's been a bit of a shock. I withdraw that remark, sir. But I assure you, you've been misinformed. I give you my word, Chang hasn't bribed me. I—er—I've been a bit too friendly with him, perhaps, but I think he's a decent chap at heart, and——"

"You'd better go, before I break your neck," Gideon said. "I don't think you're worth hanging for. As from this moment, you're relieved of all duties. You can protest to the Secretary or the Assistant Commissioner, but it won't make any difference. Stay in London, because we might want to see you at short notice."

"Look here," Foster said thickly, "at least I've got the right to speak on my own behalf."

"Every right," Gideon conceded, "and you'll get it, when the time comes. At the moment I know what you've done but I can't prove it in court. I'm going to look for proof at a time when I've a hundred other urgent jobs that need doing. I'm going to have to waste time on a job like this, and perhaps a murderer or two will get away as a result of it. That ought to make you feel happy."

Foster said thinly: "You can't prove what isn't true."

"That's right, too," said Gideon. He closed his eyes for a moment, as if he were very tired. "All right, get out."

Foster turned towards the door. With his fingers on the handle, he hesitated, and glanced over his shoulder. Gideon was no longer looking at him, but out of the window which overlooked the many windows of a wall on the other side of the rectangular yard.

But he spoke.

"Foster," he asked, "what made you do it?"

"I didn't do it," Foster said, viciously angry. "You'll be wasting your time all right. Be careful what you say, or I'll get you for defamation of character."

He went out, and slammed the door.

CHAPTER TWO

GIDEON WALKS

LEMAITRE sat on the edge of his desk, bony legs crossed, cigarette drooping from his lips. All this was safe now, as the rage was spent. As he listened, he thought that Gideon was tired and showing signs of more years than forty-nine. It was always a strain, being a Yard officer, and Gideon took his responsibilities more to heart than most. He lived his job day and night, in the office, in London, in his home. They all did, up to a point, but few so thoroughly as Gideon.

"The filthy swine," Lemaitre said, at last. "I never did like him, he's always been too smooth. Can you pin it on him?"

"Not yet," said Gideon. He was pulling at his empty pipe, a rough-surfaced cherry wood, which was almost a sign of affectation.

"Who put in the squeal?"

"Birdy."

"Well," Lemaitre said, "you can trust Birdy."

"That's right," agreed Gideon, "you can trust Birdy, especially on a job like this. His own daughter got to like reefers, and he buried her at nineteen. She'd been a pro for three years, and a dopey for two. That makes Birdy the most valuable contact man we've got in the Square Mile on all kinds of dope peddling, and we can't afford to lose him. So I've put a man on to him, and had him warned that he must look out for trouble. Because Foster will tell Chang, and Chang will try to find out who squeaked. He may not have any luck, but if he does—well, we won't go any further than that. Chang will clean up the Chang Club, too, after this morning you'll be able to run a vacuum cleaner over it and not find a grain of marihuana or any kind of dope."

"He'll do that," agreed Lemaitre. "That's what puzzles me, George. Why did you smack Foster down when you did? Why didn't you raid the place first? You might have picked Chang up and put him inside for ten years." He looked puzzled, but he grinned. "But being you, there's a reason, you cunning old so-and-so." That he could talk so freely was conclusive proof that he felt sure that Gideon was his normal calm self again. "After the suppliers?"

"Partly," Gideon said. "I went for Foster and took the chance of warning Chang because I want to drive Foster into doing something decisive. He'll have to go to Chang, if they're watched closely they'll probably be seen together. And we need proof."

Lemaitre wrinkled his nose.

"Sounds more like me talking than you," he remarked. "Couldn't you have watched Foster, without telling him what you suspected?"

Gideon let himself smile, for the first time that day.

"I've had Foster watched for two months," he said, "and even you didn't know. Got nowhere. The thing that got me this morning was the dope. I can understand a man having his palm oiled, but——" he broke off, and ruminated. Then: "I also think Chang's big time, and on his way to the top. I'd like to watch him now that he's had a smack, and see how he tries to cope."

"Cunning as a fox," Lemaitre mocked. "I'd be inclined to put him away before he became big time."

"That way, we wouldn't know who was climbing in his place," said Gideon. Unexpectedly, he smiled again; it gave him the kind of look that all his children loved to see. "You may be right, Lem, this could be one of my mistakes. I think I've started something, and I'd like to see where it goes."

"Going to report Foster to the A.C.?"

"Unofficially," Gideon said. "We can't make a charge. Foster will soon discover that, and he's bound to resign. He's got the makings of a very bad man in him. Can't possibly give him a second chance, of course, if he won't go by himself, we'll have to find a way of getting rid of him, but I don't think that will cause any trouble. Now, what's in this morning?"

He turned to his desk and the three files.

All Scotland Yard knew that the wrath was past, having spent itself on the sleek head of Detective-Sergeant Foster; none found it in themselves to be sorry, because Foster, being a know-all, was without close friends. One or two casual friends tried to pump him, without success, and he left the Yard a little after eleven o'clock.

By that time Gideon had run through the three groups of cases. *Inquiries Proceeding* held his attention more than either of the others, and he skimmed through the new cases quickly. Nothing seemed of exceptional interest. Inquiries into several robberies in central London looked like petering out, a jealous ex-lover had thrown vitriol over his love, a woman had been found murdered in Soho; the newspapers would make a sensation of it, but as far as a woman could ask for murder, she had. There was a forgery job building up; it might become very big before it was finished, but he needn't worry about that now.

The *Inquiries Proceeding* took most of his time, and the report he studied longest was one on the last mail van job, now ten days old. If the Yard had an Achilles' heel, it was that; mail van robberies had been going on for three years, and there was plenty of evidence to show that it was the work of one group of crooks; there was nothing about their identity. That worried Gideon because it had become a challenge to the Yard's prestige as well as to its skill.

It wasn't the only challenge.

There was the constant one, of drugs. Close up one distribution centre, and another would open. Judging from what he now knew, at least twelve were open all the time. None of them was big, none threatened to become extensive or to affect the lives of many people except those who were already on the fringe of crime; it was a kind of running sore. Sooner or later, a Duke's daughter or an M.P.'s son would become an addict, and then it would be made into a sensation; the Yard would be prodded from all sides, and Gideon would get as many of the prods as most. He seldom revolted against this form of injustice, for he knew well what some people seemed unable to grasp.

There was a never-ending war between the police and the criminals, a war fought with thoroughness, skill, patience and cunning on each side.

With a few exceptions, the big cases were not the important ones in this unending war. A man who had never committed a crime in his life might suddenly commit murder and his trial become a *cause célèbre*, but the chief impact upon the Yard would be to take detectives away from the daily struggle against vice and crime.

Now and again Gideon would say all this, earnestly, to a friend or to a new policeman or even a newspaper reporter, and shake his head a little sadly when he realized that they took very little notice.

There was dope, then; there were the mail van robberies; there were the thieves who worked as industriously as any man at his job or profession, taking the risk of a spell of prison life as another might take the risk of bankruptcy. Crime never stopped. Big robberies and little robberies, big thieves and the little sneaks, a few gangs but little violence, one fence sent to jail here, another discovered there—oh, the trouble with being an officer at Scotland Yard was that one lived in a tiny world, and found it hard to realize that ninety-nine per cent. of the nation's citizens were wholly law-abiding. Gideon's greatest worry, and constant anxiety, was the formidable and increasing evidence that many law-abiding people would readily become law-breakers if they had a good chance and believed that they would not be found out.

Foster was a painful case in point. . . .

Inwardly, Gideon was worried in case he had been swayed too much by his fury when handling Foster. Ninety-nine times out of a hundred he would have waited to cool off before tackling the man; this time he hadn't been able to. Every now and again he erupted as he had this morning into a rage which perhaps only he knew was virtually uncontrollable.

Well, it was done. With twenty-odd years' experience of the Square Mile behind him, he could afford to play what some people would regard as a hunch—this time, that it was wise not to pull Chang in. It was policy to keep hunches even from Lemaitre and certainly from the Assistant Commissioner, although sometimes he thought that the A.C. knew.

The A.C. took the report on Foster very well. No eruption of shock and shame, just a calm acceptance of the fact that they'd picked a bad one when they'd taken Foster, and an almost casual:

"Sure of your facts, Gideon?"

"Yes."

"All right, let me know if you think he's going to try to whitewash himself." The A.C. didn't smile, but was almost bland. "Nothing else outsize?"

"Not really," said Gideon. "Four of those mail bags were found floating in the Thames last night—from the Middlebury Road job, by the markings, when they stole the van and all. Ten days ago. Just a chance that we might be able to find out where they were thrown into the river, the River coppers are trying that now. Otherwise——" Gideon shrugged.

"If there's a job I want to finish before I get moved on, it's the mail van job," the A.C. said quietly, "but I needn't badger you about it, I know how you feel. All right, go off after your bad men." This time he smiled, and then added as Gideon stood up: "How did that girl of yours get on with her examination?"

Gideon brightened perceptibly.

"Oh, she got through, thanks. She says she was lucky, she happened to know most of the questions, but——"

"Modest, like her father," observed the A.C. "Guildhall School of Music, wasn't it? I had a niece who used to think she could play the piano, too. Your girl a pianist?"

"Fiddler," said Gideon. "Can't say I'm a devotee of the violin, but she passed her exam. all right and can take a job to-morrow—if she can get one! Won't do her any harm to find that jobs don't grow on trees, though. Hard to believe that there's a musician in the family," Gideon went on, with barely subdued pride, "I can't sing a note without being flat, and my wife—well, never mind. Will you be in to-day, if I need you?"

"I'll be at lunch from twelve-thirty to three."

Gideon kept a straight face. "Right, sir, thanks." He went out, letting the door close silently behind him, and shook his head. "Two and a half hours for lunch, and I'll be lucky if I have time to get a bowl of soup and a sandwich from the canteen." But he said it in no resentful mood; if changing incomes with the A.C. meant changing jobs, he would stay as he was. Nice of the old boy to remember Pru. Well done, Pru. Eighteen . . .

He remembered Birdy's daughter, buried at nineteen. He remembered how easy it was to become in need of reefers or of any drugs; you might have your first taste without knowing it, but you'd still be eager for a second, anxious for a third, desperate for a fourth—and there were precious few cures from addiction.

At half-past eleven, he was walking from the Yard into Parliament Street, soon to turn right towards Whitehall and Trafalgar Square. It was a crisp morning in April, no rain was about, the look of spring was upon London and the feel of spring was in Londoners. In a vague sort of way, Gideon knew that he loved London and after a fashion, loved Londoners. It wasn't just sentiment; he belonged to the hard pavements, the smell of petrol and oil, the rumble and the growl of traffic and the unending sound of footsteps, as some men belonged to the country. They could be said to love the soil. The only time that Gideon was really uneasy was when he had a job to handle outside London or one of the big cities. The country hadn't the same feel; he felt that it could cheat him, without him knowing it, whereas here in London the odds were always even.

He walked almost ponderously, six feet two in spite of slightly rounded shoulders, broad and striking enough to make most people look at him twice, and some turn and stare. He was sufficiently well-known for a dozen men to nudge their companions and say: "There's Gideon of the Yard," and sufficiently well-liked and trusted to get a grin and a "Hi, Guv'nor!" from the newspaper sellers and one or two familiars who knew him in the way of business. Very few people disliked Gideon, even among those he put inside. That was one of the reassuring things, and it put the seal to his oneness with London. He supposed, in a way, that it was the common touch. He could think the same way as many of these men thought; they were as dependent on the throbbing heart of London as he.

Dope, gangs, thieves, murderers, prostitutes, pimps, ponces, forgers, blackmailers, coiners, con-men, big-time crooks and little squealers, frightened men and terrified women, vengeful old lags like Birdy who had suffered from the parasitic growth he had helped to put upon the body of London. Here they were, all together, practitioners of every kind of crime, side by side with every kind of goodness, clean crime and "dirt", too. Somewhere, Foster was licking his wounds or talking to Chang or plotting revenge out of his hurt vanity.

Nothing happened that hadn't happened before.

Now, Gideon was going on his "daily" rounds; in fact he could afford the time to do this only once or twice each week, and the years had taught him as well as those who employed him that the time he spent on his rounds was well-spent indeed. He was going without any specific purpose, and he didn't think about Foster or crooks all the time. Twice, a young girl he passed, bright with the beauty of youth and touched with the eagerness of innocence, reminded him of his Prudence. Once he told himself that he thought more of Pru than he did of Kate, and supposed that all couples who had been married for twenty-six years lost—something.

When he got back to the Yard, it was just after twelve. Except that he had shown himself to many people who needed reminding that he was about, it had not been an eventful morning. For the past hour he had hardly given Foster a thought, which meant that his fears of having used bad tactics didn't go very deep; it would be all right.

Two or three senior officers made cryptic remarks as he went along the wide corridors, but it was Lemaitre who waited with the stunning news.

"Hallo, George, you heard?"

Gideon put his hat on a corner peg. "Heard what?"

"Foster's dead," Lemaitre said. "Run over by a car that didn't stop."

CHAPTER THREE

FOSTER'S SISTER

GIDEON did not answer as he went round to his chair, moved it gently so that the back did not scrape against the wall, and sat down. He picked up his cold pipe, and ran his fingers over the corrugations in the cherry bark. Lemaitre waited until he was sitting back, before adding:

"They rang up from Great Marlborough Street, full of it."

There was another long pause. Then: "What beats me," said Gideon, making himself keep very matter-of-fact, "is that anyone could knock a chap down in London and drive off and get away with it. Or did anyone pick up the number of the car?"

"No," said Lemaitre. "Well, not yet."

Gideon picked up a pencil, and spoke as he wrote down his first note, which read: "General call for anyone who saw moving car near fatal spot." Aloud: "Was he killed instantaneously?"

"Pretty well."

"Anything else?"

Lemaitre looked at a clock with big dark hands on the wall over the fireplace. It was ten past twelve.

"I should say it happened at eleven fifty-five," he said. "If you ask me——"

"In a minute, Lem," Gideon said, and pulled a telephone towards him, then asked for the Chief Inspectors' room, then gave instructions: it was simply a call to find witnesses of the accident, all the usual routine; he said everything in a tone which was almost eager, suggesting that these hoary measures were fresh, interesting, even exciting. "And let me know what you get, will you?" he added, and put the receiver down. "What's that, Lem?"

"If you ask me," repeated Lemaitre, "Foster telephoned Chang, Chang got the wind up, and put him away. And don't tell me I'm romancing, they don't come any worse than Chang. Just because we've never been able to put him inside, it doesn't mean that he's a lily-white——"

"All right," Gideon said, still feeling the rough bowl of the pipe, "I know all about Chang. I'd like to find out if he did know about Foster being suspended—hmm. I think I'll go myself. Wonder what time Chang gets up." He was muttering, might almost have forgotten that Lemaitre was still in the office with him. "Hell of a thing to happen. Could have committed suicide, I suppose, or else been so steamed up that he didn't look where he was going. Car didn't stop, though. Looks ugly." He stood up, thrusting both hands into the baggy pockets of his jacket, still holding the pipe in his left hand. "Anything else in?"

"Nothing much. There was a go at a mail van in Liverpool Street at half-past ten, the railway police stopped their little game, but the three men involved got away."

Gideon's interest in that seemed sharper than it had in the news of Foster's death.

"Description?"

"No. Masked, until they'd got away."

"You know, Lem," said Gideon, "if we had as much nerve as some of these johnnies, maybe we'd get results quicker. They're quick, they're smart and they're full of guts. That the lot?"

"All that matters, I think," said Lemaitre. "There's a flash about a girl's body found in an apartment near Park Lane, nothing known yet—could be natural causes or accident. Patrol car flash, just before you came in."

"Um," said Gideon. "Well, let me know." He went to the door.

"George," said Lemaitre, strongly.

"Yes?"

"Be careful with Chang."

Gideon's slatey eyes lost their brooding look, and for a moment he smiled.

"Don't be a blurry fool," he said, "snow wouldn't melt in Chang's mouth to-day, never mind about butter!" He gave that quick, paternal smile again, and went out.

On his way for the morning perambulation, he had gone almost ponderously. Now he wasn't exactly brisk, but took long strides and passed three plainclothes men moving smartly towards the lift. He reached it first.

"Hear about that mail van attempt at Liverpool Street?" asked one of them, a middle-aged detective-inspector.

"Yes," answered Gideon briefly.

A white-haired detective-sergeant said: "I've got another six months in this cowshed, and if there's a job I'd like to see finished, it's the mail van job. How many robberies is it now?"

The D.I. said: "Draw it mild. This wasn't one."

"Not often they miss."

"Thirty-nine in three years and two months," said Gideon, "and don't ask me whether they're all organized by the same man. I don't know. But I'll bet some of them are. Picked up some of the bags from the last job in the Thames," he went on, in the way he had of talking freely to subordinates whenever it was possible. "They make pretty sure we can't trace 'em back, don't they?"

"They'll slip up," the D.I. prophesied.

Gideon rubbed his chin. "It wouldn't worry me if we caught 'em before they slip up," he said. "Nice if our results weren't always governed by frailties on the part of the crooks, wouldn't it, boys?"

He sounded positively paternal.

The lift stopped, and the others made room for him to get out first.

"Thanks," he murmured, and was walking towards the steps and his car a moment later, apparently forgetful of the others.

They watched him.

"Funny thing," the elderly sergeant said, "he came in on the rampage this morning, Foster went off with a flea in his ear, and now Foster's been run down. Next thing you know, Gee-Gee will be blaming himself for it."

Gideon—his Christian name of George made Gee-Gee inevitable—squeezed into his shiny car, turned on the ignition and let in the clutch, reversed until he could swing clear, nodded to the two men who saluted him, and drove at a moderate pace on to the Embankment. He turned right, heading for Whitehall, then Trafalgar Square, then Lower Regent Street—the main road route to Great Marlborough Street. Inside the car he looked massive, and rather dull. His driving was automatic, yet he wasn't careless and was usually a move ahead of other traffic; he changed gear smoothly, and gave no sign that he was thinking about Foster.

He was wondering whether this would have happened if he hadn't blown his top with Foster. The earlier, uneasy fears—that he might have done the wrong thing—were darker and heavier in one way, worrying him. In another, he was relieved. There was no longer the certainty of scandal, the newspaper headlines, sneers at the Yard, and God knew, things were difficult enough without that. Still, it was a worry. It did not harass him enough to make him careless, or forgetful of the main task: to find out whether Lemaitre's guess was anywhere near the truth. He found himself thinking of Lemaitre with a reluctant kind of disapproval. Over the years, Lem had made the same kind of mistakes, due to impetuosity. "If you ask me, he telephoned Chang, Chang got the wind up, and put him away." Lemaitre was still capable of talking like that without a tittle of evidence, of looking upon a possibility as if it were a probability. The years of being proved wrong hadn't cured him; it was why he would never become a Superintendent, either at the Yard or one of the Divisions.

Never mind Lem!

Gideon stopped at the police station in Great Marlborough Street, and had a word with the Divisional Superintendent by telephone from the duty sergeant's desk. Nothing more was known about Foster's accident, no news had come in about the car. The body was at the morgue attached to the police station.

"Want to have a look at him?" the Station Superintendent asked. It was on the tip of Gideon's tongue to say "no", and then he changed his mind.

"Yes, thanks, mind if I go in on my own? I'm in a hurry."

"Help yourself," the other said.

There were two other bodies in the morgue; only one light was on, over a stone bench where one man lay and two others worked. Gideon moved among the stone-topped benches, until he reached the working men, and saw that Foster lay there. They'd almost finished, and didn't look up until one of them drew a white sheet over Foster's body, up as far as the chin. From where Gideon stood, he had a foreshortened view of Foster; he realized that he had been a strikingly good-looking man.

One of the others, a police-surgeon with black hair and a bald patch, looked up.

"Hallo, George."

" 'Lo, Harry."

"He went out as quick and clean as a whistle," said the police-surgeon, "it's always a help when you know that. Cracked the back of his head, and crushed his stomach, but the face is hardly damaged. Worked with you sometimes, didn't he?"

Gideon nodded.

"Married?" asked the police-surgeon.

"No," said Gideon. "One sister, no other close relatives." Asked about any of the men who worked with him regularly, he could have given an answer as promptly and as accurately. "Well, there we are." He turned away, and walked with the police-surgeon towards the door of the morgue.

They didn't say much.

Back in his car, Gideon waited long enough to pack the pipe loosely with a mixture, and to light it. Two loose pipes in the morning, two in the afternoon and as many as he wanted in the evening, was his rule. He brushed a speck of glowing tobacco off his trousers, then moved off.

It wasn't far from here to Winter Street, Soho, where Chang had his club.

There was no room to park. Gideon drove round twice and then spotted a constable.

"I'm going to leave this here, double-parked," he said. "Keep an eye open, and if it blocks anyone who wants to get out, move it for me." He took it for granted that he was recognized, handed over his ignition key, and walked towards Chang's, which was just round the corner.

For a district in the heart of the biggest city in the world, this was a disgrace and degradation. It was almost the only part of London Gideon disliked. The buildings were mostly dilapidated, none was impressive; it was like a shopping centre in the East End, except for the masses of cars parked bumper to bumper. Most of the shops looked closed. A laundry, a shop advertising: "*We make new collars from shirt tails*"; a butcher's shop open, with a woman with brassy hair and talon-like red nails smoking a cigarette and talking to the butcher, showed a glimpse of Soho life as it really was. Gideon knew the woman; she'd been up before the magistrate at Great Marlborough or Bow Street regularly for the past twenty years. She lived close by, and bought her groceries, her meat, her milk, all the things of daily life, from these small shops. Well, why not? She had to live somewhere. A corner shop was filled with dark-haired men and women, all shorter than the average Londoner; they were southern French, Italian or Spanish—and mostly Italian, Gideon knew. In the windows on the shelves were delicacies brought from the ends of the earth—literally from the ends of the earth. If you wanted a speciality of the Chinese, the Japanese, the Javanese, of India, Brazil, the south of Spain or the north of Italy, from Yugoslavia or from Russia, you could buy it here. Inside, everyone was chatting, all were dressed in black, and Gideon scented a funeral party preparing for the meal to come.

The pavements were dusty, the gutters littered with chaff, pieces of paper, cigarette ends, bus tickets. Dust carts and street sweepers could come through Soho half a dozen times a day without ridding it of this hint of squalor in the worst streets; and Winter Street was one of the worst.

By day, Chang's looked harmless.

The name, in mock-Chinese lettering, was on the fascia board, and the weather or years had worn it so badly that most of the "h" and part of the "g" were obliterated. Chang had been here a long time. It was a double-fronted shop, and the windows were blotted out with dirty-looking muslin curtains, but the *Bill of Fare*, showing what Chang had to offer in an English hand which would have suited a Billingsgate pub, looked clean enough. It was a restaurant by day and club by night.

Gideon went in.

He knew that he had been seen approaching; probably when he had driven past here he had been recognized. Word spread in Soho as quickly as it did to the Yard. He knew that the broad smile on the face of the diminutive Chinese who came towards him, hands covered in the folds of his snow-white apron, hair shiny with oil and expression one of friendliness and delight, could hide anything from thoughts of murder to honest curiosity.

"Goodday, sa, you like good lunch?"

"No, thanks," Gideon said. "Is Chang in?"

"Chang, sa?" The slit eyes widened, the hands performed strange gyrations, still beneath the apron. "I find out, sa, name please?"

"Gideon," said Gideon. "Never mind, I'll find out for myself."

He walked across the sawdusted boards, past several Chinese eating English food, a Malayan couple eating rice and an Indian woman in a pale pink sari, sitting in front of a metal tray with several metal dishes on it, and pushed open a door. Beyond was the kitchen; this was spotlessly clean, with two Chinese women working in the steamy heat. Beyond again was a staircase. Gideon went up the staircase, without hurrying. The boy would have warned Chang.

Gideon sniffed.

There was a strong smell of paint, and it became more noticeable as he approached the landing. The narrow stairs creaked. A strip of hair carpet ran in the middle of them, and along both passages at the top. One door, closed, was marked: "*Office*". The other door, open, was marked: "*Club*". "Club" had never been more than a name used so as to obtain a late liquor licence, and until recently Chang had done nothing to invite being closed up.

Two painters were busy in the club room, one lanky Englishman with a sniff, the other a sturdy, handsome

youngster, obviously not English.   "A Pole," Gideon
thought, as he spoke to the lanky man.

"When you'd start this job?"

Wary, watery eyes turned towards him.

"S'morning."

"When did you get the order?"

The lanky man's eyes were now narrowed so tightly that
they were nearly closed. The Pole was working steadily,
using a small brush fat with crimson paint. The big club-
room stank of oil paint and distemper.

Gideon heard the other door open, although it made little
sound.

"None-of-yer-bus'ness," the lanky man drawled nasally.

Gideon didn't argue. "I'll know you again," he said, and
turned round.

He wasn't surprised to see Chang in the office doorway.
He was surprised to see the woman behind him, standing up
and looking somehow unsure of herself, like someone who'd
had an unpleasant surprise. She was quite a good-looker,
and Gideon knew and had once danced with her at a police
ball.

She was Foster's sister, and her name was Flo.

CHAPTER FOUR

CHANG

CHANG was smiling diffidently.

Flo Foster wasn't really smiling at all, just looking bewildered. Gideon did not start guessing what she was doing here; it was better to find out for certain. He felt sure that something Chang had said, perhaps about his arrival, had startled her. She was not the type to look bewildered for long, and Gideon had another thought, the kind he would pigeon-hole and bring out for examination whenever he felt it necessary. Only a sharp shock would have affected her like this. She came from the same world and had much the same poise—over-confidence—as Foster himself. He did not know her well enough to wonder whether she had the same capacity for error as Foster. Error was one word! He judged that she was quite free from the taint of drugs, heavy drinking or any kind of debauchery; she looked not only handsome but wholesome and healthy. She was undoubtedly touched with arrogance.

All this took only a second or two to pass through Gideon's mind.

Chang was moving forward, hands held a little in front of his chest in a gesture which was already self-deprecatory. He had a big, wide forehead and a small, shallow chin, and his face tapered down in the proper proportions from his forehead. One first noticed that, which was smooth as yellowed alabaster, and then his small ears, which stuck out almost at right angles and seemed to thrust a way through his dark hair; hair, like that of most Chinese, as straight as a woman's in need of a perm. The rest of Chang was not, perhaps, important. He had the facial characteristics of the oriental, but only those who knew the Orient well could have said whether he was Chinese, Javanese, or one of the other races. His small mouth was faintly pink; a dirty pink.

His eyes were dark and pinched a little at the corners; that didn't stop them from being blackly bright. His nose was slightly flattened and the nostrils were dark. For the rest, he was beautifully tailored in pale grey, with a discreet blue tie, a blue handkerchief making a triangle in his breast pocket and, almost certainly, blue socks to match.

He was not effusive. His English was good, with more inflection than accent. He had been born within five miles of this spot, and knew no other language; but he could use pidgin English effectively at times, and pretend not to know English fluently.

"Mr. Gideon," he said, "how unexpected. A pleasure indeed." Now, his hands touched at the tips, and he gave the slightest of bows. "You are most welcome. I was about to show my previous visitor the stairs, you will forgive me?"

"That's all right," Gideon said.

"Perhaps you will wait here for me." Chang thrust a hand, fingers crooked and palm upwards, towards his office, showing the natural grace so many of his kind had. His smile was not overdone.

"This way, please," he said to Foster's sister, and stepped in front of Gideon, making no bones about wanting the woman to go.

Gideon showed no sign of recognition. Flo Foster now looked away from him, and moved quickly, as if anxious to get out of his sight. She looked good, but not necessarily in the sense of goodness. Her two-piece suit of rust-colour serge fitted well, and she had all black accessories—gloves, bag, shoes—with a touch of quality.

Gideon inclined his head, ponderously.

When Chang had started down the stairs with Flo Foster, Gideon went into the office. He left the door open. The lanky painter was staring at him, his brush hanging in the air; the Pole was still working, now on distemper with a big brush. Gideon didn't sit down, but stepped to the window and then to a spot out of sight from the surly painter. He touched nothing, but looked about him quickly and intently, missing little. Gideon was a man who, playing the parlour game of "what were the articles on that tray" would invariably win, and would seldom miss even a single item. All he saw here were a few papers, neatly arranged, a big locked safe in one corner, a carved sandalwood box containing cigarettes. The desk was a cheap walnut pedestal one, with a tubular steel swivel chair behind it, and a square of brown carpet centred on the floor had a green linoleum surround.

Chang came back quietly, shut the door and hid the English painter. He smiled with the familiar reserve, and went round to his chair. His hand moved out again.

"Please sit down."

"Thanks." Gideon sat on an upright chair which looked and felt too flimsy for him. He did not say that he had recognized Foster's sister. Chang's expression was bland; his lips didn't close completely, and showed a glint of white teeth. The silence and the protracted stare probably put him on edge, but nothing in this world was likely to make him show it.

"What can I do for you, Superintendent?"

"Has Foster been here to-day?" Gideon asked, flatly.

"Foster, Superintendent? Who is Foster?"

"You know," said Gideon.

"I am afraid that I do not understand," Chang declared. "Foster, Foster." He let the name float in the air, and so declared his tactics: flat denial of everything. He did not know Foster, he had never bribed Foster, he had not heard that day from anyone named Foster. At the end of this series of mute denials there was defiance, as evident although as mute: "And you cannot prove that I know Foster."

Gideon was convinced that Chang knew everything, now felt that he could go all the way with Lemaitre, although there was still no evidence. By his denials, Chang not only showed his hand but also made it clear that he did not think there was anything to worry about.

Confidence had always been his strong suit.

Over-confidence? Like Foster.

Gideon said: "I mean Eric Foster, a detective-sergeant at New Scotland Yard, who's been taking money from you for some time, Chang."

"It is some mistake," said Chang, very smoothly. "Perhaps you forget I am not the only Chang in Soho, Mr. Superintendent."

"No," admitted Gideon, "I don't forget." He changed the subject but not his tone. "What are you having the club-room painted for?"

"But *that*?" asked Chang, and smiled now with greater readiness; a stranger, seeing him for the first time, would have been greatly struck by his open face, the apparently friendly smile, the charm. "I have many clients and I do very well, Mr. Superintendent, and so I am giving them something more pleasant than before."

Gideon didn't answer. Chang did not wilt or even waver slightly under the ruthless scrutiny.

"Chang," said Gideon, suddenly, heavily, "I want to tell you a thing or two. In this country, crimes catch up with you. You ought to know that. Murderers get hanged, thieves get jailed, all criminals get punished sooner or later. We may miss them on one job but we always get them on another. Don't ever think you're safe. You've been doing some of the foulest things a man can do, and we're after you. That means we'll get you."

Chang's smile became broader, although perhaps it grew a little tense.

"It is a pity," he said carefully. "I have always liked to be friends with the police. And I shall always be ready to be friends, Mr. Superintendent, but now you talk in hostile mysteries. How can *I* help?"

"You can't help yourself or us," Gideon declared flatly. "You've gone too far." He got up and moved towards the door, wondering whether to use his only bullet or whether to keep it. He used it: "Who was that woman in here just now?"

"My visitor?" Chang was not even slightly perturbed. "A charming lady, one Mrs. Addinson. She is a painter who would have liked to paint the walls of the club but—" he gave a charming little shrug—"she would also like too much money!" He moved towards Gideon, fingertips touching. "So nice to have seen you again, Mr. Superintendent, I hope soon we shall be friends once more."

The smell of paint was almost overpowering on the landing. The lanky painter had lit a fresh cigarette, and seemed to be pouring thinners into a tin of paint. The Pole was slapping distemper on to the ceiling, standing on a square packing case in order to reach up. Gideon didn't look at Chang again, but went deliberately downstairs, glanced into the kitchen, was escorted to the street door by the grinning youth, whose hands still hid themselves beneath the snow-white apron.

Gideon walked back to his car. The policeman was at hand eager to be of help.

"Have you seen Birdy Merrick about to-day?" asked Gideon.

"No, sir, haven't set eyes on him."

"Well, if you do, tell him to keep out of Chang's reach for a bit," said Gideon. "Noticed anything unusual at Chang's to-day?"

"Well—in a way, sir."

"What way?"

"He had a visitor—a nice-looking young lady, sir. He often has visitors, but not that kind and they don't usually come in the morning, they're nightbirds. Saw her at his window. She's left now, sir. "

"Hmm. Thanks. Anything else?"

"No, sir, but then I've been on my rounds most of the time."

"Any friends round here who might know what's been going on at Chang's?"

"I think I could get someone to tell us, sir."

"Get them to, will you? Who left Chang's place this morning after eleven o'clock, say. Especially anyone with a tough reputation. Chang knows plenty of them."

The constable said worriedly: "They *usually* come at night, sir. It's not easy to recognize them."

"We're looking for the exception," said Gideon, and smiled to encourage. "Always worth trying. G'bye."

He got in his car, but didn't drive off immediately. Instead, he picked up the radio-telephone, flicked it on, waited for the humming sound to tell him it was alive, then called the Yard. The man who answered from the Information Room knew his voice.

"Yes, sir, two messages for you. One of the three men who tried to rob a mail van at Liverpool Street Station this morning is under charge, being brought to the Yard now, sir—should be here in ten minutes or so. The child found dead in Hatherley Court, London, W.1 was murdered—strangled and interfered with, sir. Chief Inspector Suter has gone over there, and will report as soon as he's had a look round. That's all, sir."

"Hmm," said Gideon. His nose was wrinkled, his mouth turned down at the corners. Most men had a secret horror, his was of men who could first ravage and then kill a child. Nothing, not even the Changs with their dope and devilry, could make him see red so quickly, and as always, he distrusted himself when he saw red. "All right, I'll come straight back."

"Very good, sir."

Gideon started off. At the corners, men and women loitered. The first of the pro's were beginning their ambling, more people were in the shops, a brewer's dray with a big engine instead of the horses of yesteryear stood outside a pub while barrels were dropped down the chute into the cellar. A normal enough scene.

Gideon began to feel angry about that child and sour because he couldn't go straight to see Florence Foster. She had to be told about her brother. The job would be left to the Yard, and he couldn't see anyone else doing it willingly. He found himself thinking again that if he hadn't torn Foster to shreds in the office, it might not have happened. It was that blurry hunch—the kind of thing he'd dress Lemaitre down for, but there it was. The Square Mile was his beat, and some pulsating sixth sense told him that this wasn't the time to go for Chang, but the time to start squeezing. When you squeezed a slug, it was surprising what oozed out. Chang with his diffident smile, his charm, his courtesy and grace, with as foul a mind——

Gideon slid through the traffic and began to argue with himself.

Half the trouble with men like Chang, whether they were Chinese, English or American—it didn't matter what nationality they were—was that they had no sense of doing wrong. They were as the slave traders had been a century ago, as the white slavers of North Africa were to-day. To them, nothing was sacred, nothing inviolate. He knew of a dozen men, respected, wealthy, perfectly honest by the legal codes, who rejected all moral values.

Foster had said the thing all these would say: if girls didn't get dope from Chang, they would get it from someone else. So, it was no crime to make money out of giving it to them. Orientals especially seemed to lack a sense of morality, but, hell, some of them were pretty strict in applying moral rules to their own families. That wasn't the point. The point, Gideon decided as he turned carefully into the gateway of Scotland Yard, was that most Eastern countries bred a lot of callousness, the people were fatalists, and if they came to England and turned against the law they were deadly because usually they had good minds and no scruples.

"Something," Gideon said suddenly and aloud, "in a Christian civilization." And then he scowled. "Still, what about Foster?"

He parked the car with more room to spare, and went up the steps. If he cared to count the number of times a week he went up those steps, he would be astounded. Some Superintendents spent most of their time at the desk; some people said he didn't spend enough. He didn't trouble about the lift, but went up the stairs two at a time, nodding at the many who passed him. His own office was empty, a disappointment. Before he sat down, he pressed a bell for a sergeant. Then he dropped heavily into his chair, and squinted down at a pencilled note Lemaitre had left:

"Mail job man's talking, main waiting room. Lem."

There was a tap at the door and a sergeant in plainclothes came in, absurdly young in Gideon's eyes.

"Yes, sir?"

"Get the Secretary's file on Detective-Sergeant Foster, will you? Put it on my desk. Check whether his sister, Florence, still lives with him. Lived. If she has a place of her own, find out where it is, find out where she worked, what she does. Don't take too much time about it. See if you can pick up anything from the other sergeants in Foster's office."

"I could put up a bit myself, sir."

Gideon, looking through other messages as he talked, glanced up into grey, eager eyes.

"All right, Miller, what?"

"Still lives—lived—with his sister, sir. I was on a job with him two days ago, he was moan—he was saying that he would have to get a place of his own, his sister didn't like his off duty hours. He was a bit tetchy. I gathered he'd had a row with her."

"Hmm. Anything else?"

"They live Chelsea way."

"Yes. Check everything you can. Thanks, Miller. If I'm wanted I'll be in the waiting-room with that mail van chap." Gideon nodded and hurried out, thinking of the Fosters quarrelling and Flo Foster's (Addinson's) surprise, and a man who'd tried to rob a mail van being in talkative mood.

The main waiting-room was on the floor below. Gideon was there in thirty seconds, and opened the door briskly. He heard the words of a man speaking in a cultured voice:

". . . I tell you that's all I know!"

The speaker was young, probably in his late teens. Take away his thin mouth, and he would be a nice-looking lad, with fair, curly hair, cornflower blue eyes, a look of innocence; full of a kind of charm, like Chang. As he stared at the door, he looked scared, and caught his breath sharply at sight of Gideon's burly figure. Lemaitre and two sergeants were in the room with the youth; one was from Liverpool Street, the other a Yard man taking notes. The youth was neatly dressed, well-groomed.

"Anything?" asked Gideon.

"Nothing that won't bear repeating," Lemaitre said, "and I should say he's conveniently forgetting a hell of a lot."

"That's a lie!" the youth burst out.

"All right, calm down," said Gideon. He looked at the prisoner's fingers, stained dark with nicotine, then at the thin, unsteady mouth, and wondered when Lemaitre was going to grow up. He took out a fat, old-fashioned silver cigarette case and proffered it; the youth grabbed, as some kids would grab a reefer. He snatched a lighter out of his pocket.

"Thanks." He drew fiercely.

"That's all right," said Gideon, "no need to get steamed up, it won't make any difference, and if you play your cards right you'll probably get off more lightly than you deserve. Mind telling me all about it again?"

In the pause which followed, he glanced at the sergeant's notebook, and read the name: Lionel Tenby.

"Well, Tenby," he went on, in an almost comforting way. "What about it?"

"I've told them!" The words came with a rush, a spate followed. "I don't know the names of the others, it was all laid on by telephone. They knew I could drive a damned sight better than most chaps, so they paid me twenty-five quid to do this job for them. All I had to do was to drive up in front of the van and wait until they told me to get a move on."

"Payment in advance?" asked Gideon.

"Yes." Tenby's gaze flickered towards a table where oddments lay in neat array; a pocket-watch, a comb, wallet, keys, silver coins, copper coins and a small wad of one pound notes.

Gideon's hopes began to fade; this wasn't the first time they'd caught a very small sprat.

"And you didn't know them?"

"No."

"Pity. What else?"

"I asked them how they knew it would be worth doing, and they said that someone had tipped them the wink," Tenby declared. The cigarette was nearly finished, and he seemed to look at it anxiously, as if nervous of what he would feel like when he had to stub it out.

"Tip from where?" asked Gideon.

"How the devil should I know?"

"Hmm," said Gideon. Yes, it was disappointing. If things went on like this, it was going to be an unsatisfactory day. "All right, get that statement typed out, sergeant, have

Tenby read it and if he agrees that it's what he said, have him sign it." He looked at Tenby patiently. "But don't sign it and then start squealing to the magistrate that it isn't what you said. If you're not satisfied, write it out yourself in longhand."

Tenby winced—because the cigarette, now burned very low, stung his fingers.

Gideon gave him another.

"Throw the stub in the fireplace," he said. "You can have some cigarettes. It'll be deducted from any money belonging to you. Fix it, sergeant."

"Yes, sir."

"Anyone you want to know about this?" Gideon asked sharply.

Tenby's eyes glistened; he was very young and he wasn't one of the bad ones—just a young fool.

"No."

"Girl-friend? Parents? "

"*No!*"

"Been in before on a charge?"

"No, I—I wish to God I'd never listened to those swine! I'd dropped a bit on the gees, and——" he broke off, biting his lips. Bring his mother into the room at this moment and he would burst into tears, Gideon surmised.

"Well, listen," Gideon said, "your relations have got to know, and it's better from us than from the Press, you won't get much change out of the Press. Let us tell your parents or the girl-friend, and have them——"

"*I said no!*"

"All right. Let him suffer. Come on, Lem," Gideon said, and led the way out. "Not much there," he added almost absently. "The story we've had a dozen times before. The P.O. people pick their drivers well. Like to know if it's directed by one man or not, there's a lot of similarity. When he's calmed down a bit, get repeat descriptions of the two men. Play him soft, though. Get hold of his people, if you can, and let them come and see him here. Mother, preferably. Blurry young fool." He changed the subject but didn't alter his tone of voice. "Hear about the Mayfair flat job?"

"Nine-year-old kid," said Lemaitre. "I could tell you
what I'd do to them if I had my way."

"Thing that worries me with those jobs is the risk of
another," Gideon said. "We really want to bring the house
down after the chap."

"I'll say!"

"I'd better go along to the Back Room," Gideon said, as if
he wasn't quite sure. "The Press will be on their toes. If
they play up the child murder and the frustrated mail van
robbery, they won't have much room for anything else."
They were at a corner, where they would go different ways.
"Saw Chang, by the way. Smooth as ever, denies everything." He didn't say anything about Flo Foster (Addinson). "And the club-room there is being redecorated. The
smell of paint and distemper makes sure that no one with a
sensitive nose could ever pick out the marihuana they've
been smoking."

"You know what you've done, don't you?" Lemaitre said,
with a sniff.

"What?"

"Driven Chang somewhere else. It won't stop the kids
from getting the weed, and——"

"Nearest thing I know to a certainty is that Chang won't do
anything he shouldn't for some time," Gideon asserted,
marvelling that Lemaitre should think anything different.
What limitations even able men had! "We could draw all our
dogs off him and he'd still behave like a learner priest,
what-do-you-call-'em? Acolyte, isn't it? It's beginning to
look as if he did hear from Foster, and got a move on. Might
have had a row with Foster, though, and so made Foster
walk across the road in a rage, not looking. Nobody ever
thinks they could be knocked down in a street accident."

"The car didn't stop," Lemaitre insisted. "Don't you
want to believe that——"

Gideon was suddenly sharp; almost harsh.

"No," he said bluntly. "No, *I don't* want to believe that
Chang had Foster killed. I don't want to think that Foster
knew so much about Chang that it was worth killing him.
But that's probably what happened, and if it is we'll get the

killer and we'll get Chang!" He switched abruptly. "Any news in?"

"We've picked up a girl typist who was looking out of the window and says she saw it happen. She was on her own, her boss was out, and when she saw someone come along the street to Foster's help, she just sat back."

Gideon flashed: "Any squeal of brakes?"

"Eh?"

"Did she hear—never mind, where is she?"

"On her way here."

"Oh, good," said Gideon, "that's fine. By the way, there's a painter chap at Chang's, very thin, six-feet one or two, big Adam's apple, watery eyes, probably blind or half-blind in the right, it's hazed over. Flat-footed, and pretty sly. I'd like his name and address and anything we can find out about him. There's a copper on duty over there, P.C. 10952. He seemed to have his head screwed on the right way and he's finding out if anything worth knowing happened at Chang's this morning. Send someone out to have a word with him about this painter."

"Okay," said Lemaitre.

They were outside the office. Lemaitre opened the door and Gideon went inside, looking at the carpet and giving a little frown, one more of preoccupation than of annoyance or worry.

"Well, we didn't get much out of the mail van chap," Lemaitre said. "Nearly always the same, if we do pick anyone up it's a young fool who doesn't know anything. But there was a tip-off again, that's the worrying thing, George, isn't it?"

"Hm?"

"A tip-off from the post office."

"Oh, yes."

"I'll tell you what's going to happen one of these days," said Lemaitre. "They're going to kill a copper or someone who tries to stop them and then our noses are going to be rubbed right in the dirt." His own thin nose wrinkled disgustedly. "Anything goes wrong, they blame us, but whose fault are these mail van jobs? We're understaffed, could do with dozens more at every station in London. The P.O. don't use half enough detectives—seem to think that every van is protected by some spirit."

"Okay, Lem," Gideon said. "It's everybody's fault but ours, and we've got the job of stopping it."

He sat down at his desk, grunting.

On it was a note—a pencilled report on an official buff form.

> Telephone message received from 7Q Division
> 12.55 p.m.
> Killer of nine-year-old Jennifer Gay Lee at Hatherley Court believed to be Arthur Sayer of 15, Warrender Street, Ealing. Ealing Division has been telephoned, general call asked for Sayer, description and photograph on way to us by special messenger.

Lemaitre was standing by the desk, looking down.

"What's this?"

"Old Tucker at 7Q thinks he can name the swine who killed that kid," said Gideon. "As soon as the photograph and description arrive, put out a general call, ports, airfields, everything, just for safety's sake. I wish——"

The telephone bell rang.

"Gideon," he grunted into it, and then brightened. "That's good. Keep her down there, the small waiting-room, I'll come and see her at once." He put the receiver down. "It's that typist who saw Foster knocked down. If she heard a squeal of brakes the driver tried to stop; if she didn't, there's the evidence you've been looking for." He gave Lemaitre a quick but rather tired grin, and went out.

Two minutes later, there was a tap at the door. A constable in uniform, except that he was hatless, came in.

"Photograph and description from 7Q Division, sir."

"Okay, I'll have 'em," Lemaitre said. He stretched out a hand, and a moment later looked down at the glossy photograph of a man. "So that's the brute, is it? Okay, ta."

Lemaitre picked up a telephone and started to put out the

general call for a certain Arthur Sayer, who was believed to have murdered the nine-year-old girl. As he talked into the telephone he skimmed the report of the murder, and his eyes frosted, even his tone changed, because it was a very, very ugly killing.

". . . . and get a move on," he said. "Once that kind's tasted blood you never know where they'll stop."

The door opened, and Gideon came in, eyes bright, manner brisk, as if he were beginning to relish life.

"Seen her?" Lemaitre asked needlessly.

"Nice little kid, a bit scared, but reliable. There was no squeal of brakes, there's the pointer we want, Lem. Was probably intentional. Anything else in?"

That was like a refrain.

"No," said Lemaitre, "but that poor kid . . ." He was brief but graphic in his description of the mutilations on a child's body.

Gideon stood in the middle of the office, like a statue rough-hewn out of granite.

"Schools are closed for the Easter holidays," he said abruptly. "Sayer knew this child, and she trusted him. Better check on other children he knows, fast. All right. I'll talk to Ealing."

He almost threw himself at the telephone on his desk.

CHAPTER FIVE

THE CHILD KILLER

CHILDREN swarmed over Clapham Common. Every square yard of grass was worn bare; every yard of the children's gravelled playground with its swings and seesaws, sliding chutes and vaulting horses, had a pair of feet—well shod, rough shod, badly shod, even three children who were bare-footed and wearing such rags that others looked at them askance, and some refused to play.

Clapham Common was one of the places where London breathed.

Now, at the tail-end of the Easter holidays, mothers were only too glad to shoo their offspring out. The morning had echoed with the same refrains in a thousand doorways and kitchens: "Be careful crossing the road." "Don't go getting yourself dirty." "No fighting, mind." "Don't speak to any strange man, understand?" "Look both ways." The children had listened with half an ear, and found their way safely towards this breathing ground, soon racing, rushing, running, sprawling, giggling, laughing, crying, climbing, shouting, shrieking in the warm air of late spring.

Here, youths of recognized local renown chose sides at cricket or at football, coats went down for goal-posts or wickets, bats came out after a winter's storage, footballs looked flat and flabby and gave off a dull sound when kicked, and stubbed strong toes.

On the seats round the edges of the common, the old folk sat, mostly nice, pleasant, sleepy and indulgent, some with a packet of peppermints or toffees, most of the men with pipe and a little tobacco, all drowsy in the sun and the din. A few of these were nasty old men, but each was known by the common keepers, the local police, and by a few self-appointed guardians of the children.

"Nothing," each harassed mother had said or thought

when the children had gone flying down the road, "can happen to them once they're on the common." And most watched until the first roads were crossed and then went to wash-tub, sink, floors or bedrooms, or dressed hastily to go out shopping, gradually forgetting fears which would only return if the children were back late for the mid-day meal.

A few knew that their children might be late, most knew that hunger would bring them clattering home, a few minutes before one o'clock, or before half-past one; whichever was the regular meal time.

Of these, Mrs. Lucy Saparelli was one.

Mrs. Saparelli, at thirty-seven, was a red-cheeked, bright-eyed, wholesome-looking woman with a spruce figure and a seductive walk, although she had no idea that a few of the louts of the district called her Marilyn. Her husband was a commercial traveller away three or four nights out of the week's seven. He had only a vague notion that his forebears had been Spanish or Italian, and wasn't quite sure which. He could go back four generations of solid English ancestry, but was oddly proud of his unusual name. *Sap*-ar-elli.

He loved and trusted his wife and he was fiercely fond of Michael, his eldest child and as fond of Dorothy, his youngest —aged nine—although for some reason, Victor, the eleven-year-old who came in between, always managed to irritate him.

Victor did not irritate his mother, but if one of the apples of her eyes was brighter than the others, it was Dorothy. Boys drew away from their mother as the years passed, but Dorothy would always be with her. At nine, she was—just *lovely*. She had the looks, the plumpness, the *naïveté* and the natural gaiety which could make a child win approval from everyone. The hug that Lucy Saparelli gave Dorothy each night and each morning was born of the little extra delight the child gave her. Delight was the word which mattered, was the thing the girl child brought to Lucy, to Jim Saparelli, to the two boys.

Everyone loved Dorothy.

Arthur Sayer *loved* Dorothy.

Arthur Sayer knew the Saparellis well, because he had lodged with them some years ago, a schooldays acquaintance of Jim's who had been welcome when money had been short. It had soon become apparent that he was ever so nice, except for one thing: betting was his folly. Lucy had been heard to say, almost in tones of wonder, that he never said a word or put a finger out of place. He was rather odd, in some ways, a bit cissy, with long, silky, brown hair and a love of bright colours, but—well, nice.

Lucy was in her bedroom, scurrying round to make the beds and dust before going to the shops, when the front door bell rang.

"Damn!" she said, and looked out of the window, but saw no van; so it wasn't a tradesman. She peeked at herself in the mirror and straightened her hair as she hurried down the stairs, her skirt riding up over her pretty legs. The dress was a little too tight and one she only wore when doing the house-work. She went quickly along the stained boards of the hall, seeing the dark shadow of a man against the coloured glass panels in the top of the door. She knew it was a man because of the shape of his hat.

It was then ten o'clock on Gideon's day; when Gideon was still at the Yard looking at reports.

Lucy opened the door.

"Why, Arthur!" she exclaimed, and annoyance faded in pleasure. "Fancy seeing you at this hour of the morning. Come in, do."

Arthur Sayer hesitated, and she stared at him intently.

He was almost one of the family, and more welcome than most of her in-laws. He looked pale, and his eyes glittered, as if his head ached badly; she remembered that he had often had severe headaches, needing absolute quiet to recover from them. He needed a shave, now, and his coat collar was turned up, although it was already warm.

"*You* look as if you've been up all night," said Lucy forth-rightly. "You'd better let me make you a cup of tea and give you some aspirins."

He moved forward.

"Thank—thanks, Lucy. I've got one of my awful head-aches."

"Why on earth didn't you stay at home?"

He moistened his lips.

"I—I had a row with someone," he said. "Never mind about that now. I—I knew you'd let me rest here for a bit."

"So I should think!" said Lucy. "Look, you go in the front room, draw the blinds, and sit quiet until I bring you a cuppa." She thrust open the door of the parlour. "The only things in there are Dorothy's dolls, she's having her friends in to an exhibition. That child and her dolls! Now, sit you down, I won't be a couple of jiffs."

She left him in the darkened room.

She frowned as she walked to the kitchen, every movement touched with throbbing vitality. She filled the kettle, put it on the gas, washed two cups and saucers from the pile waiting from breakfast, and then shook her head with a quick little gesture.

"The rest'll have to wait until after lunch. I can do all the washing-up together. Now he's come I can't get everything finished before I go out." A pause. "I suppose I *must* go out?"

She put the question aloud, but answered it silently. She gave Arthur very little thought as a person, just accepted him as she accepted the ups and downs of family life, the aches and pains of her children. Had Arthur been one of hers, she would have felt worried because he didn't look well; but she'd seen him almost as bad, it wasn't very important.

Jim would be home to-night, and she liked to have a good dinner for him, so she *must* go to the butcher's. If she had to go out she might just as well do all the week-end shopping and get it over. She would finish the bedrooms before she left. . . .

If Dorothy came back while she was out, Arthur could let her in, she wouldn't have to play in the street.

She bustled round, easy in her mind.

Arthur said very little when she took in the tea, but swallowed three aspirins obediently. His eyes were glittery, and she wondered if he was running a temperature. Dorothy always went pale when she had a temperature, and the boys were usually flushed.

"Sure you'll be all right on your own, Arthur?"

"Yes—yes, thank you."

"Wouldn't like to see a doctor?"

"No!" He almost shouted the word. "No, don't—don't tell anyone I'm here."

"Look here," said Lucy flatly, "what's upset you, Art? You can confide in me, you know. What's the trouble?"

"Nothing! I—well, I—I owe some money, Lucy, I can get it back, but——"

"Why didn't you say so? It isn't as if it's the first time." Lucy sniffed. "I won't tell anyone you're here, and Jim's coming home to-night, perhaps he can suggest something to help. Now I've got to go to the shops. You needn't answer the door if you don't want to, but if Dorothy comes back I don't like her playing out in the street. Let her in, won't you?"

Arthur Sayer didn't answer.

"Art, you might at least answer me!"

"Oh," said Sayer. "What did—oh, yes. Yes, I'll let Dorothy in. Don't worry, Lucy."

She left him alone, but was uneasy in her mind—although not because of Dorothy. That did not occur to her. He had helped to nurse Dorothy, was Uncle Art to her and would be for the rest of her life. She sensed that he was in serious trouble, and came of stock which was easily embarrassed by thought of any trouble which might warrant the interest of the police. Arthur had always been silly with money and that gambling, but——

She saw a bus coming along the main road as soon as she reached it, and rushed across to catch it. Some drivers would wait, some were *devils*.

She caught the bus. The only spare seat was next to a girl with a horse's tail tied with pink ribbon, who was reading the *Daily Mirror* . . .

Dorothy Saparelli stumbled away from the swing, and the hard wooden edge caught her a slight glancing blow on the shoulder. She turned and shook her fist at the bigger girl who had just grabbed the chain, and had made her get off. Nine years is not the age when one admits the justice of accusations of wrong-doing. She had used that swing for fifteen minutes and wanted it for another fifteen.

She brushed back some hair which had somehow escaped from one of the sleek wings which seemed to sweep from a centre parting. It was black, glossy hair, tied with scarlet ribbon. She wore a white blouse and a navy blue gym suit, her plimsols were dusty but not dirty or torn.

"Mean pig!" she called shrilly, and looked disconsolate.

Three children were clinging to every place where there was room for one; on this playground Dorothy hadn't a chance of another toy. She sauntered over to a group of girls playing rounders, but they were in the early teens, and one snapped her fingers and ordered:

"You sheer off."

Further afield, Victor was playing football. She couldn't see Michael, who was probably messing about at cricket. Disgruntled, a little tired and very thirsty, Dorothy made her way along a tarred path towards the roads leading to Micklem Street, where she lived. There was only one main road to worry about, but she could cope with that; when in doubt, wait until grown-ups were going to cross, and cross with them. That was so much part of training that a child's pride was never challenged; it simply wasn't safe to cross on one's own.

An old man, carrying a walking stick, was coming towards her.

She didn't like him, and moved off the path, but he stood and watched, raising his stick and smiling invitingly. He had no teeth, and a funny, straggly kind of moustache and beard. She saw him take a bag of peppermints out of his pocket, and it seemed as if her mother's voice was actually sounding in her ears.

"*Never stop and talk to strange men, even if they do offer you sweets.*"

She skipped past this old man. She wasn't really troubled, and the moment she was past him, he was forgotten, as a dog safely behind a gate would be. It did not occur to her that the uniformed policeman who started to hurry in the wake of the old man was doing so because of that little interlude.

One word of early warning could save a lot of distress.

Dorothy crossed the main road safely behind a woman with a push-chair.

She loitered on her way to the house.

She was happier here, her troubles quite forgotten, when a black-and-white spaniel puppy frisked up. She was almost outside her own house, Number 24, when she saw a sixpence glistening on the pavement.

A tanner!

She pounced.

Her delight, as she looked at it on the palm of her hand, was the absolute delight of a young child. Her whole world had changed. She held a fortune because this was money she had not dreamed she would have.

There was a corner sweet-shop, not far off.

She hesitated, wondering whether to go and spend her find, or whether to tell her mother. Mum would let her keep it, she was sure of that: findings keepings, if you really *had* found it. Seeing a few dirty marks on it, she began to rub the sixpence with the forefinger of her left hand. She looked at the front room window. The curtains were drawn, but there was a little gap in the middle.

She did not see Arthur Sayer looking at her.

She was *very* thirsty.

She went to the front door, at a hop, skip and jump pace, and banged on the iron knocker. She hoped Mum was in because she was so thirsty, but if she wasn't Mrs. Pommery next door would let her have a drink of water, or—should she buy a *lemonade*? Excitement rose again. She imagined the sharp sweetness of aerated lemonade on her cloyed mouth, and the temptation was so great that she wished she hadn't knocked. If Mum was out——

The door opened.

Arthur Sayer opened the door.

Dorothy stared, and then her eyes glowed.

"Why, Uncle *Arthur*!"

She went in gaily, and he closed the door behind her, heard her chattering, heard the story of the sixpence, followed her to the kitchen, watched her turn on the tap and put a cup under it . . .

She screamed three times.

Mercifully, that was all.

No one heard her, except Arthur Sayer.

Lucy Saparelli got off the bus with Mrs. Pommery, who lived next door, and was the only neighbour likely to have heard a sound from the Saparellis' kitchen. Each woman carried laden baskets; Lucy Saparelli had one in each hand. Yet they walked briskly, and a spotty youth, a nightworker, lounging against the porch of his home, watched Lucy's swaying hips and gave a silent whistle, then a whispered: "Hi, Marilyn!" Lucy was talking, about the price of food, about Victor, about her Jim being a bit hard on Victor sometimes, about Dorothy's plan to have an exhibition of dolls, a kind of dolls' party, and wasn't it wonderful for a nine-year-old girl to think of such an idea on her own?

They turned the corner.

Lucy changed hands with the baskets, and wriggled her shoulders because of the strain.

Then she saw Victor and Michael, talking to another boy outside their home. She didn't give a thought to the possibility of—horror. Michael had torn his trousers, and Victor had a nasty scratch on the side of his face, but they looked clear-eyed and happy.

" 'Lo, mum!"

"Gosh, I'm hungry."

"We'll have something to eat as soon as I've had time to look round," said Lucy. "Micky, take this bag for me, there's a dear. Victor, you can open the door for me, take the key out of my bag—oh, silly ass! Just knock, and Uncle Arthur will let us in."

"What?" Michael took the laden bag. "No one's in, Mum. I've knocked half a dozen times."

"Well, that's *funny*," said Lucy. "Where's Dorothy, then?"

She didn't speak again, but opened her bag, took out the front door key, and went straight to the front door. She could not have told the others what had happened to her in that moment; she probably did not realize it herself. It was as if a shadow had fallen; a darkness, hiding something she was anxious to see. She did not consciously think of Dorothy. Afterwards, to her husband, she said in a stony voice that she thought Arthur might have done himself in.

She pushed the door open, strode in, and called: "Arthur!"

There was no reply.

She looked inside the parlour, which was empty but for the dolls. She went briskly along the passage, high heels tapping on the stained boards, with Michael behind her and Victor just stepping across the front door mat.

Then she saw . . .

Then she *screamed*.

CHAPTER SIX

MAN-HUNT

GIDEON sat at his desk, in his shirt-sleeves, the big, blue and red spotted tie undone and ends hanging down, hair ruffled, face pale but forehead damp with sweat. He had a telephone at his ear, and was waving his left hand at Lemaitre, who came across.

"Someone saw him leave on foot, just before half-past twelve, so he didn't get far. Concentrate everything we've got on the south and south-west London area. Right." He waved Lemaitre away, and grunted into the telephone: "Yes, I've got all that, thanks." He rang off, and plucked up another telephone. "Back Room," he demanded, and stretched his shoulders, leaning back so that his head touched the wall. Then, with his free hand, he picked up the first telephone again. "Is Sergeant Miller back yet? . . . Yes I'll hold on."

The Back Room Inspector spoke into the telephone at Gideon's right ear.

"Yes, George?"

"This Sayer chap," Gideon said without preamble. "Have a go at the evening paper chaps, ring up the news editors if necessary, ask them to make sure they run Sayer's picture in each edition, getting it in as soon as they can. And give 'em a picture of a girl . . . either of them will do . . . Yes, I've just had a word with the Old Man, he's okayed it. Thanks." He rang off, spoke immediately into the other telephone. "Hallo? . . . Good, send him in to me."

He put that receiver down too, and took a deep breath.

Lemaitre was holding on to a telephone, but not speaking. He looked across and said:

"We won't get any more done if we starve. What about some grub? *Hallo*. Yes, all the men you can spare, pick up photographs of Sayer at 7Q, that's the quickest way."

The door opened and the sergeant who had been instructed to find out what he could about Foster's sister, came in. He seemed touched by the vibrant excitement which affected the others. Neat as a new pin, he entered as if he were daring the lion's den, with Gideon the lion. But Gideon's expression was placid and his voice quiet, in spite of his pallor and the sweat on his forehead.

"Well, what have you got?" he asked.

"Miss Foster's at her home now," the sergeant said. "Incidentally, sir, she's married, and separated from her husband. She's a Mrs. Addinson. She does murals for cafés and night clubs, has a little studio in the Chelsea flat where they—she lives. As far as I know, she doesn't yet know what happened to Sergeant Foster."

"Chelsea, yes," said Gideon. "Hmm." He lived in Fulham, the adjoining borough. "All right, thanks." The sergeant put down some notes, and turned to go. "Sergeant, send someone down to the canteen for some sandwiches and beer for both of us. Ham and beef all right, Lem?"

Lemaitre seemed to be listening to someone on his telephone; but he nodded.

"Beef well done, and plenty of salt," ordered Gideon. "Thanks." He nodded and looked hard at the two telephones, as if he could not understand why they were silent; neither had rung for nearly five minutes. He wiped his forehead, then his neck, then made a gesture by tightening the knot of the tie, but he didn't do his shirt up at the neck. The once smooth, starched whiteness of the collar had wilted, and was damp near the neck.

Lemaitre said "Oke" into a telephone, banged down the receiver, groped for a cigarette, lit it, and glanced at Gideon. "Quiet all of a sudden, isn't it?"

"It's one of those days," Gideon said. "Two supers off duty, one ill, three out-of-town jobs taken our best C.I.'s. One of these days I'm going——"

One of his telephone bells rang.

He took it up slowly, almost gently.

"Superintendent Gideon here. Who? . . . Yes, yes, go on." His eyes glistened, he grabbed a pencil and made waving signs in the air with it. He jotted down a couple of notes, and said: "Yes, fine, thanks." He let the receiver go down with a bang, and Lemaitre, looking at him, had an odd thought: that Gideon looked ten years younger than he had first thing that morning. "The River boys say those mail bags were dropped into the Thames somewhere near Battersea Power Station. They've been out to look, and found another flapping around a submerged barge. It caught on a nail or something. Footprints near the spot, some tyre marks, everything that might help us to get something. I can push that on to B2, pity it's near the Sayer job, but still . . ." He lifted a telephone. "Give me B2 headquarters . . ." He waited, rubbing his forehead with the palm of his left hand. Then: "Hallo, Superintendent Gillick? . . . Gideon here . . . No, not Sayer, but that's priority . . . Yes, he's a swine all right . . . Listen, Gil, the River boys think that some mail bags, part of that last post office job, were thrown in the river from a spot near Battersea Power Station last night. They've a launch standing by to guide your chaps, can you spare a couple? . . . Sure, sure, plaster casts, tyre-tracks, all the usual, and if we could have them this afternoon we might catch the beggars yet. We had a set of tyre-tracks and some footprints from the Maida Vale job, you know, be interesting to see if they match up . . . Yes, thanks . . . Oh, fine, everyone of them, noisy brats most of them . . ." He shook his head at Lemaitre, who was grinning broadly, and rolled his eyes. "Yes, the oldest boy's working, thanks, doing nicely . . . Thanks a lot, Gil."

He blew out a noisy breath as he put the receiver down.

"Champion talker on the Force," Lemaitre said. "Why don't you ring off when he starts gassing like that?"

"Might want some special help from him before this is over," said Gideon philosophically, then looked up at a tap at the door. "I'll swear at anyone short of the Old Man," he declared, and barked: "Come in!"

It was the uniformed but hatless constable, with a tray, sandwiches with ham and beef overlapping the bread, and two pint bottles of beer.

"And *wel*come!" grinned Lemaitre.

Downstairs in the Information Room, uniformed men were standing by the big maps spread out on tables in front of them, with tiny model cars and other models on the tables, and croupier's rakes to move them with. There was a continual chatter of low-pitched conversation, some men talking into radio telephones, some into ordinary telephones, some to neighbours. No beehive would be busier on an early summer's day.

There were more men round one of the boards than any other—that depicting the south-west area. Here concentrations of model cars and of policemen and plainclothes men stuck on round wooden bases were continually being moved. A report would come by radio telephone, a car would be moved; a report would come by telephone, and a man moved.

All the Divisional Police Stations and the sub-stations in the south-western area of London were reporting regularly. Police in uniform and in plainclothes were calling on shopkeepers throughout the huge area, with descriptions of Arthur Sayer. Photographs, some prints hardly dry, were already being distributed in large numbers. Special forces were watching spots like Clapham Common, Battersea Park and Tooting Bec—all places where children played.

In Clapham, a Divisional Inspector with a soft Devon burr in his voice was talking to Lucy Saparelli. Lucy seemed to have shrunk, her voice was a hoarse whisper. Michael and Victor were next door with the neighbour, and a sergeant—selected because he had boys of his own—was talking to them about Sayer.

The two o'clock radio programme on all wavelengths was interrupted with a description of the wanted man. The next evening newspaper editions carried his photographs as well as photographs of the first child victim, Jennifer Gay Lee. No minute, no second of time passed without someone showing another picture of Sayer, or asking if he'd been seen in the district.

Gradually the search narrowed. Sayer had been seen at Brixton, in the biggest shopping centre in the immediate neighbourhood.

A policeman who had been travelling on a bus recognized him. He did not give chase, but went swiftly to a nearby police box and telephoned his sub-station.

"Got off near the Forum," he reported to his sergeant, "same place as I did. Looked a bit dazed, if you know what I mean."

"I'd daze him! Which way did he go?"

"Turned left—yes, that's right, left."

"Well, that's something." The sergeant picked up a telephone, and the message was flashed to the Yard. Instructions went out smoothly and swiftly for men to concentrate in the Brixton area, with the Forum cinema as a focal point.

Then a waitress at a busy café, shown the photograph by a plainclothes man, looked up at him eagerly.

"Why, he's been here!"

"Sure?"

"Course I'm sure, I served him, didn't I? Asked him if he had a headache, and he bit my head off. And a tuppenny tip! Not that I expect——"

"Which way did he go?"

"Well, I don't know that I noticed . . ."

"I know the one," said the cashier, leaning out of her box. "Wearing a light brown coat and grey flannels, and one of those pork pie hats. He turned left."

"Sure?"

"Wouldn't say so if I wasn't."

Shopkeepers, vanmen, road-sweepers, traffic duty police, newspaper sellers, newsagents—everyone between the café and the Forum was questioned quickly and comprehensively, and each revealed a little more of Sayer's trail. It always led the same way: to the Forum.

A commissionaire said: "Let's have a better look." He peered. "D'you know, I think that chap's *inside*. Come in half an hour ago. I remember he looked over his shoulder as if he were scared of being followed, that's him all right. What's he done?"

A policeman explained.

"*What?*" The commissionaire looked sick.

A cashier said nervously: "We only had about twenty in, and he was one of them. 'Course I'm sure."

"That's him all right," said the usherette on duty at the balcony entrance. "Proper cissy he looked, and his hands was so cold you wouldn't believe . . . And don't you come it, copper—just happened to touch his hands while I was tearing his ticket in half, that's all."

A sergeant in charge said: "We'll cover all the exits, then telephone H.Q."

The Superintendent at the Divisional H.Q. said: "Good, but don't go in for him yet, I'll phone the Yard."

Gideon was finishing his last sandwich when the telephone broke a glorious period of ten minutes' quiet. It rang sharply, with its oddly imperious note. He swallowed hard, washed the bread and meat down with a gulp of beer, and snatched the receiver up; he moved quickly, as if feeling guilty at having been eating for ten minutes.

"Gideon . . ."

"Put him through!"

"Hallo, Gordie . . . The Forum, Brixton? . . . Fine . . . I don't know whether he'll put up a fight or not . . . Only weapon we know he's got is that knife . . . No, I won't come over myself, much rather your chaps handled him; if he's there I'm sure you won't miss him . . . Yes, please, the moment you have any news . . . Gordie, half a mo', and don't get me wrong, he might be deadly. He'll know that he hasn't a chance to save himself from hanging, and he could be right out of his mind. I—*God !*"

Gideon broke off.

Lemaitre actually jumped out of his seat.

"Get your men inside that place," shouted Gideon, "it'll be dark inside, and there might be some kids. I'm coming."

CHAPTER SEVEN

OLD WOMAN ALONE

At about the time that Gideon was shouting into the telephone in a kind of anguish, an old woman sat alone in the parlour behind her small shop in Islington, on the other side of London.

Her name was Mrs. Annie Sharp.

The Islington police, on the look-out for Arthur Sayer, were on the look-out for a lot of other people, too, although with less urgency. None of them suspected that there was any danger for the old woman in her shop. She had lived in the two rooms at the back for thirty years, and had never been known to have a holiday. Her husband had been killed early in the first world war, and since then she had managed alone. Now, her five children were married; those neighbours who knew her well knew that only two kept in touch with her, and one of those was now in Australia.

Annie Sharp was a good-natured, friendly soul, and although the shop did not make plenitude for her, it kept her from want. The counter was built so that she could move from the sweets and chocolate side to the tobacco, matches and cigarette side without trouble, and her small till was on the corner of the counter, immediately opposite the door leading to the parlour.

The upstairs flat was let to a man, his wife and three children, but these were all out. Annie Sharp knew that, but it did not worry her; thirty years without a frightening incident in the same place breeds a kind of confidence which has nothing to do with logic or probability. The district had its tough and its rough spots, but Annie Sharp's experience with crime was limited to a few small bad debts; and although she was a kindly and soft-hearted woman, some shrewd instinct warned her not to let anyone have more than a day or so's credit.

"Don't ask for credit," said a little printed card in a fly-blown show-case, *"and you won't be refused."* That hint was effective.

The two o'clock back-to-work hooter of a nearby factory had finished blowing some time ago. Everyone who came home for lunch had gone back now. Annie knew from experience that she was in for the quietest period of the day. Until about half-past three, when the women started out with their perambulators, the most she could expect was the odd casual customer for cigarettes; or the child who had succeeded in wheedling a few coppers from a parent who was probably feeling desperately anxious to have forty winks.

The shop door-bell would wake Annie up.

She settled down, with her feet up on an old, velour-covered pouffe, her thin grey hair awry, her head resting on the back of a comfortable old wing chair. She wore carpet slippers, worn shapeless by shuffling, but in spite of her seventy-two years she had a surprisingly tight little figure.

A tap, needing a new washer, dripped in the kitchen, but the sound did not disturb her. After a few seconds, she began to snore faintly. That and the continual dripping of the water into a saucepan made the only nearby sounds. Occasionally someone walked sharply along the pavement, or a car drove past, but these were distant sounds, and did not disturb Annie Sharp.

Then the bell at the shop door clanged.

Her eyes opened, and she clutched the arms of the chair in the same instant. She allowed herself a second or two to wake, then stood up. The shop door, on a black japanned spring fastener, closed slowly.

"Coming," she called.

Then she heard a sound that worried her. It was as if the flap of the counter was being raised, and she allowed no one to come in here without being invited. A child, perhaps, trying to sneak sweets. What children were coming to . . .

She hurried to the doorway.

She saw the man.

He looked young, although it was hard to be sure of that, because he wore a cap pulled low over his eyes, and a brown scarf drawn up over the lower half of his face. He was at the till, and as she reached the door, it went *ting!* sharply.

"*Here!*" she cried, "you get out of here!" She bustled forward, more angry than scared; but a little scared too. "Go on, be off——"

"Shut up," the youth said.

She saw his narrowed eyes, and didn't like them, but she was still more angry than scared, and snatched up a bottle of Coca-Cola from a case standing on a shelf.

"Be off!" she shouted.

He didn't speak again. His voice had sounded gruff and vague behind the scarf, but there was nothing vague about his spiteful eyes. She raised the bottle, and he struck her hand aside. The bottle dropped but didn't break. He had a piece of short iron piping in his other hand; Annie Sharp saw it and opened her mouth to scream.

He struck, savagely . . .

He struck again and a third time, but the third blow wasn't really necessary.

He dragged her behind the counter and then into the little back room. Two children went hurrying past, girl and boy. He pushed the old woman in a corner, where she lay, bleeding to death, and then made a quick search. He found twenty-five pounds in an old tea caddy, and a small bundle of notes which he didn't trouble to count, in a sewing basket. He muttered something under his breath, glanced at the woman, and then went into the shop.

The till was still open.

He took the few pound and ten-shilling notes from the back, grabbed a handful of silver and dropped it into his jacket pocket, then stepped through the gap in the counter, dropped the flap and went to the door.

He pulled down the scarf, bent his head, opened the door —and almost fell over a toddler standing and peering at the sweets, spittle-damp fingers making patterns on the window. He shoved the child aside. A woman, pushing a small-wheeled pram, was coming from the right. The man turned left. The woman stopped at the shop. The killer reached a corner and looked round; the woman was putting the brake on the pram and going into the shop.

He began to run.

Gideon, with a sergeant beside him, drove down Brixton High Street as if he were on a lap at Silverstone. He succeeded in scaring the sergeant, who until then had regarded himself as fit for the Flying Squad. He seemed to shoulder other cars aside, and had an impudent disregard of the giant buses, the throbbing of petrol and diesel engines, the wayward antics of cyclists, who thought themselves danger-proof. Seeing the Forum a little way ahead, the sergeant said:

"Nearly there, sir, slow down now."

Gideon grunted.

He saw a gap in the cars parked outside the Forum, and performed a miracle of parking, getting into the space and then out of the car almost in one and the same movement.

Once out and on the pavement, the fury slackened.

A plainclothes man whom he recognized vaguely and two whom he didn't were coming out of the cinema. Several uniformed police were about them, like a blue-bottle bodyguard. Handcuffed to a man half a head taller than himself, was Arthur Sayer. His lips were parted and trembling, he was pulling against the plainclothes man, although a second man held his other arm and was helping him along.

Gideon saw the car they were heading for. He went to it. He would have confessed to no one in the world that his heart was thumping painfully, and that he hardly knew how to frame his question.

"Any more trouble?" he asked as they drew near.

The man he recognized said: "Any more—oh, more kids? No. He was sitting just behind a couple, but hadn't started anything. I—you want to talk to him, sir?" The Divisional man suddenly realized who this was and what respect was due to Gideon.

Gideon wiped his forehead.

"Not now," he said. "But we'll want him at the Yard. Better get him there at once, and have a doctor to him." He looked at Arthur Sayer with eyes which had the hardness of diamonds. "Don't stand any nonsense from him."

"Take it from me we won't, sir!"

"All right," said Gideon. He watched them squeezing into a police car, but hardly saw Sayer; he pictured two small girls, and two mothers and two fathers, some sisters and brothers. He trumpeted into his handkerchief, then turned to the sergeant whom he had scared. "Do you know Micklem Street, Clapham, Sergeant?"

"Oh, yes, sir, near the Common."

"We'll go there."

"Yes, sir."

"And this time," said Gideon, without conceding a smile, "I'll drive according to the Highway Code, you needn't hold on so tight." He got in and shot a sideways glance at the embarrassed sergeant. "Get the Yard on that radio, will you, and find out if there's anything in for me."

"Yes, sir!"

Gideon drove as a benevolent bus driver might, with far, far more than average care. He heard the sergeant asking questions. He felt a sense of satisfaction from which anxiety wasn't altogether erased. They'd got Sayer, and with luck they'd hang him. The blurry psychological quacks would try to prove that he was insane, though. Gideon could see the shape of their case for the defence already.

He ought to have told that man what doctor to send for.

"Sergeant, tell them that Sayer is on his way——"

"I have, sir."

"And will they keep all doctors away from him and hold off questioning until Dr. Page-Henderson or Dr. Julian Forsyth can examine him. Ask them to pass that request through to the Old—to the A.C."

"Yes, sir."

The sergeant obeyed, and then listened to the radio reports.

"Anything for me?" asked Gideon.

"They've got that tyre and footprint cast ready at B2 Division," said the sergeant. "Superintendent Gillick asked whether you'd happen to be passing, so that you could pop in and have a word for him."

Gideon stifled a groan, and then said:

"I'll see."

The sergeant directed him to the street where Lucy Saparelli lived. Judging from the crowds at either end, the throngs on the pavement, the cars parked in or near the street, more people were drawn here than by a street accident, and that was saying something. In spite of police help when they recognized him, Gideon couldn't drive right up to the house. When he squeezed out of the shiny car, a battery of newspapermen, many with cameras, came towards him like a moving phalanx. It was almost automatic: ask questions, take photographs with flashlights which brightened even the bright day, and then hurl more questions.

"All right," Gideon said, "we've got Sayer, you can go home and write your story."

They flung their questions . . .

After two minutes, Gideon pushed his way through towards the front door of Lucy Saparelli's house. He had some idea of what he would find behind the door now closed and guarded by a policeman in uniform. He was not duty-bound to see the mother of the murdered child, yet something urged him to; as it had from the moment of seeing Sayer captured.

The constable had a key.

Gideon went in.

Two women were with Mrs. Saparelli, there were teapots and kettles and cups and saucers everywhere, untidy as a child's toys. People spoke to Gideon but he wasn't interested until he saw the mother. He stood, a giant in the small room, and looked at her, remembering. It was an old story and a long one, and it still hurt. Kate had asked him not to go on duty, but to telephone an excuse, because their second child was ill. He'd brushed the suggestion off, and told her to pull herself together.

The child had died during the night. One of seven, so six were left; but the gap was still there.

A mother, bereaved, looked like a woman robbed of hope. Kate had; Lucy Saparelli did.

"I just came to tell you," Gideon said, looking into those strange lack-lustre eyes, "that we've caught him."

"Have you?" Her voice was strained; empty.

"Yes, Mrs. Saparelli. We made quite sure of that. Is there anything we can do to help? Your husband——"

"No," she said, "you've been ever so good, all of you police have, and Jim's on his way." She didn't look at Gideon as she spoke. "Ever so good," she repeated, "but there's nothing anyone can do, now, nothing anyone can do."

Gideon knew that she wasn't going to cry. He knew that it was going to be much worse with her than with many women. Kate hadn't cried. He didn't know why, but he sensed a measure of self-reproach, of self-blame, in Mrs. Saparelli. He made a mental note to tell a police-surgeon to have a word with the woman's doctor about that, as he said good-bye.

It hadn't taken long but he was glad that he had been, even though it made him feel more vicious. It wasn't only the crime; the actual offence for which a man might hang or serve a long term of imprisonment, was not the really deadly thing. That, a living evil, was the effect on those who suffered. Mrs. Saparelli, with the long years of self-reproach ahead, was now living in the shadow of death, and thinking: "If only I'd done this . . ."

It was always the same; there was so much suffering; that was why he hated killers.

The sergeant was at the side of his car, speaking into the walkie-talkie.

"Anything fresh?" asked Gideon, flatly.

"Old woman's been attacked, Islington way," said the sergeant. He might have been reporting a case of shoplifting, judging from his voice. "Alone in a shop—till robbed—she was battered to death."

"Death?"

"Yes, sir."

"Oh, hell," breathed Gideon. "Hell." It was almost a groan.

"There was an attempted mail van robbery at Cannon Street station twenty minutes ago," the sergeant went on in exactly the same voice. "No one's been caught but there's a description of the driver of a van, and the car's been held."

Gideon straightened his back. Something happened to him; something quite wonderful; as if he'd taken a tonic, which had instantaneous effect. His dull eyes brightened.

"Where? Cannon Street?"

"Yes, sir."

"Well, well," said Gideon. "Two of the devils stopped in one day, eh? That's not so bad, not bad at all, we're improving." The dark shadows vanished completely from his eyes, there was eager brightness in them as he rounded the nose of the car and took the wheel. "Might get those beggars soon, after all."

He was looking ahead; to Gillick, to the tyre and footprint casts, and to the time when he would be able to include in his report one murderer caught and two mail van robberies averted.

Behind him, there was grief.

About him, there were the crimes being plotted and the criminals preparing; the good and the bad. He did not always realize how wearying it was to deal almost exclusively with the bad.

Two young men whom Gideon did not know, and of whom he had never heard, were preparing to play a part in his life at the time that he left the Yard to visit Superintendent Gillick. Neither knew that they would cross Gideon's path, although one realized that there was a serious risk that he would run into trouble with the police.

The name of the first was Alec Fitzroy. He was twenty-seven years old, had a small West End flat, and a private income of about five hundred pounds a year which wasn't anything like enough for his expensive tastes or his gambling debts. For a long time he had pondered on ways and means of making a fortune quickly, and had come to the conclusion that the most likely way was by theft.

He had two cronies whose names don't matter.

The name of the second man was Julian Small. He too was twenty-seven years old, lived in two small rooms close to the church near the river, and not far from Shipham's Café, and also had a private income of about five hundred pounds a

year. The stipend from his curacy at St. Mary's brought in
an additional two hundred pounds a year. Of his total income
he spent one-half on his personal needs, and the rest on the
needs of the church and the needy of the parish, especially
on the Youth Club. He had only been in the parish for a few
months. The Vicar was venerable and frail, known to everyone in the district rather as a piece of furniture is known in a
home. No one ever took any notice of him at all.

A great many people took notice of Julian Small. He was
unhappily possessed of a long, thin nose which was always
red. He looked weedy, too, and he took little trouble with his
clothes. After the first few weeks, the boys with whom he had
tried to cope had discovered that he was not gifted with the
necessary authority. He was full of high hopes and good
intentions, but was so easily guyed.

Many were cruel, and guyed him.

Julian Small had one thing in common with Alec Fitzroy:
education. They had, in fact, been educated at the same
school, and had left in the same year. Their background was
as nearly identical as a background could be. One had a
widowed mother, the other a widower-father.

In every other way they were almost unbelievably different; but they did have similar thoughts that day although the
one was heavy-hearted and bitterly resigned, the other was
vicious and determined at all costs to get the money he
needed.

Julian Small, walking from his flat to the church, turned
into the tiny churchyard and the headstones grimed by
London's sooty atmosphere, and kicked against a piece of
string tied to headstones and stretching across the path. He
crashed down. He tried to save his nose, but couldn't; the
blow on it was so painful that tears of pain sprang to his eyes.
They were not only of pain as he picked himself up and
walked blindly along the path towards the church doors.
Shrill, cruel laughter followed him, and brought shame and
despair to quicken the tears. He was a failure; nothing could
ever alter the fact. There were times when he felt that he
almost *hated* the people in the district; the children.

"Suffer the little children . . ."

Some of these were devils!

They shouted obscenities after him, and roared with laughter until the heavy door closed on him. They might go away. They might raid the churchyard. They might throw stones through the windows; the stained glass had long since been moved, for it wasn't safe. There was no end to the sacrileges that the children would commit and which many of their parents would condone.

Julian Small was probably the unhappiest man in the East End of London that morning, and when he looked into a small mirror and saw the blood welling up at the end of his nose, he raised clenched fists and shook them at the reflection that he hated as much as he hated the children.

Or some of them . . .

Alec Fitzroy wept no tears of pain or vexation. At the time when Small was pitching forward on to the asphalt of the churchyard path, Fitzroy was in the upper safe deposit of the Mid-Union Safe Deposit Company, in Wattle Street, E.C.3. He had rented a deed-box there a few months ago, when the plan he was expecting to put into operation to-night had first taken shape in his mind.

He had met a youngster, now one of his cronies, who had been fired by the Mid-Union for drinking when on night duty; and the idea had been born then. Since that night Fitzroy had learned all he could about the safe deposit, the upper room and the main vaults; and he had studied the system by which it was staffed and run at night. His crony had given him a great deal of help.

Fitzroy believed that his plot was almost foolproof. All it needed was a strong nerve. He had that; so had his two accomplices, one of them a man whom Fitzroy had met in the Air Force and who lived in much the same way as Fitzroy; lazily, lustfully, greedily.

Fitzroy telephoned each man to tell him that this was to be the night, and to lay everything on. That was the first direct move in the collision which was coming with Gideon.

Gideon was on his way across the river, to see Gillick.

CHAPTER EIGHT

TYREPRINT

GILLICK was a big block of a man with a heavy, thrusting jaw and a peculiarly small mouth with a short upper lip. When he talked, he appeared to be chewing, and to his cost Gideon knew that Gillick talked a lot. There was no better man on detail in the whole of London, including the Yard, and his failing was his touchiness. When annoyed, and it was easy to annoy him, he could and often would fall back on working strictly to regulation, and on no job in the world were go-slow tactics more exasperating. The days when the Yard asked for urgent information by open postcard had gone at last, but Gillick knew every regulation that he could use so as to be unhelpful.

His big, pedestal desk was so tidy that it didn't seem real. He stood up from it, navy blue reefer coat open and square corners brushing a single file of papers, a thick red hand held out.

"Hallo, Gee-Gee, haven't seen you for years! Well, months! Nice day. Must say you're looking well. Got that child killer, I hear; quick work, good job we have a bit of luck sometimes. Pity about Foster, nasty job when a man like Foster gets knocked over. What was he doing—making an arrest, d'you think?"

Gillick paused; and his little brown eyes probed, obviously he thought he was on to something.

"Not been suggested, old man," Gideon said comfortably. "I'll have another look at the reports, though. You might have something there."

"Never know," said Gillick warningly. "Fresh mind often helps." He went off again, each sentence short and the pause after each one barely noticeable. Any other man would have sounded breathless, but not Gillick. "Two mail van jobs stopped to-day, I see—don't say we're really near at last.

Talking about that, these prints. Footprints not much good. Look."

Some white plaster of Paris casts stood on a trestle table against one wall. On each was a card, neatly typewritten, giving the details. There were seven casts of footprints, but only one of a complete toe, another of a complete heel. The card near the toe read:

> Footprint, man's right toe, found in mud on South Bank of River Thames, Battersea, spot identifiable as three hundred and fifty (350) yards from the main loading jetty of the Battersea Power Station.

> Note indentation showing sole sprigged (nailed) on, not sewn. Note smooth edge suggesting plenty of wear.

Gideon studied all these, well aware that Gillick was keeping the most important until the last.

"By the way, old man," said Gillick, "like a spot? Not too late? Oh, well, cuppa tea? Good, I'll send for it." He picked up a telephone and gave orders as a martinet would. "Won't be long." He broke off and turned to the trestle. "Tyreprint's better, now. See." He picked up a large glossy print, showing the tyre track, the footprints, other signs of activity on the river bank; it was an excellent photograph, and showed where a car or light van had driven over a soft patch of sandy soil; the mark of the tyre couldn't have been made more clearly in plaster of Paris itself. "Michelin make, and that's something, they don't make a lot of small tyres, this was a 5.50 x 16. Almost new, too—see how sharp that impression is?"

He now turned to the prize exhibit—the moulded cast of the tyre. It was beautifully made, quite an artist's job.

"You've got a good chap on this stuff," Gideon said.

"Training, my boy, that's the answer—training! Beat hell out of them every time they turn in a rough job, and they soon stop. It's really something, this is. Any other make of tyre and it would be needle in haystack, but Michelin of this size—eh?"

Gideon felt his pulse quickening, in spite of almost instinctive disagreement with anything that Gillick said.

"You're right, Gil," he said, "this may really be something. It doesn't square up with the other track we got, that was a Dunlop, but we can get a search made for this." If there were a job in the calendar which really made him feel deeply at any given moment, it was the mail van job. Hope of results could always excite. "How many photographs have you got?"

"Dozen. Twelve. To spare, I mean."

"Casts?"

"Three. Two each for you, one for my own Black Museum." Gillick grinned; his little mouth didn't stretch very widely.

There was a tap at the door.

"There's the tea," Gillick said. "Well, hope this bit of work gets us somewhere. Can't say we lost any time . . ."

Twenty minutes later, Gideon left the B2 Headquarters, with Gillick purring, and the casts loaded into the boot of Gideon's Wolseley. He had spoken to Lemaitre by telephone and details of the Michelin tyre were being teleprinted for attention by all London and Home Counties Stations; the quiet, methodical, thorough search for it would begin before dark and go on all to-morrow and for days on end; the eyes of every policeman would be cast down, and every Michelin tyre would be suspect. It wasn't really much; but the owners of cars with 5.50 x 16 Michelins could be watched, and their movements checked; and if a thousand, if ten thousand discreet inquiries proved fruitless and futile, there might be one which helped.

The Yard sergeant came hurrying out of the station, wiping his hand across the back of his mouth; there were two or three cake crumbs on his sleeve.

"You had any lunch?" Gideon asked abruptly.

"Just managed a bite, sir, I'm all right."

"Hmm. Well, I'm going to look in at home for half an hour, hardly recognize the place when I do get there."

The sergeant smiled, dutifully.

"So you drive back to the Yard, get this stuff unloaded,

tell the boys to be careful with it, and then come back for me."

"Yes, sir."

They drove over Battersea Bridge, then turned left instead of right—which they would take for the Yard. Gideon took off his hat and enjoyed the cold wind stinging his forehead. He felt too hot in his serge coat and waistcoat; now he came to think, it had been getting hotter since mid-day and must be near the seventies.

He wondered if Kate would be in. He knew quite well that he wanted to have a cup of tea with her because of the look in Lucy Saparelli's eyes. He wondered whether Kate would be pleased to see him; the youngsters would—no, the youngsters wouldn't!

The three girls were out at a party—Prudence to play in the glow of her examination success, Priscilla to recite, no doubt—she was a wonderful mimic. Well, good. Penelope just to look pretty, and no one could do that more easily.

Pretty Penelope.

Pretty, dead Dorothy Saparelli and Jennifer Gay—what was the first dead girl's name? He couldn't call it to mind.

Prudence eighteen plus, Priscilla fifteen plus, Penelope twelve, with Pru younger than her years except in her playing, so they were all good friends. There was a greater disparity in the ages of the boys. Tom, the oldest, was twenty-six, Matthew was fourteen, Malcolm only just eight. Matthew would almost certainly be out playing—he'd probably gone as far as Putney Common, or even to Wimbledon. Malcolm was more likely to be at home with Kate—unless she had taken him out.

Well, at least he'd have looked in.

The sergeant got out of the car to open the door for him. "Thanks," said Gideon. He did not consciously make a note of the man's name or the way he'd behaved, but except for that attack of nerves when Gideon had been driving, he'd done very well. Shorter than most, wiry fair hair, slim waist and no hips to speak of, he was quick-moving, quiet, efficient; oh, yes, and his name was Wedderburn.

"Oh, come straight back. I've got another call to make."

"Right, sir."

Harringdon Street, Fulham, was on the "classy" side, north of the Wandsworth Bridge Road, near Hurlingham—still an oddly exclusive district although bordered by some of the poorer neighbourhoods of south-west London. The solid houses were all of red brick, two storey plus attic, and most of the householders were sufficiently well off to keep them in good repair; painting the outside every third year was a matter of pride. This had been Gideon's third year, and the painting had been finished only a few weeks ago. It was still bright and shiny, black and white as Kate had wanted it, and made him look up with interest and satisfaction; one could still take pleasure in the appearance of one's house.

There were two stone steps, a shallow porch, and a solid oak door—the door put in by Gideon. Most front doors in Harringdon Street had coloured glass panels, open invitation to light-fingered gentry.

Not that wood would keep anyone out, if he wanted to get in.

There was a small front garden, neat and attractive, with a postage stamp lawn, two beds of vari-coloured wallflowers, daffodils out and tulips not yet in flower. No one was about; the street as well as the house looked empty. Gideon felt a twinge of disappointment, but it wasn't very strong.

They had come to live in the upstairs flat here when he and Kate had married, and over the years they had converted the flats to one house, reversing the usual process. Always handy with his tools and not so busy in those early days as he had been for the last ten years, he had worked on the attic so as to make a roomy playroom and cubicles for the boys. Now Tom had a small room to himself, and the younger boys the cubicles. A corner of the playroom was used for their books and homework.

Pru had now a tiny partitioned room to herself; the younger girls shared the other side of the partition.

Gideon took out his keys, opened the door, and wondered when he had last come back during daylight. Three Sundays ago, when all the family had been waiting for him since noon, a job had cropped up . . .

The hall was narrow but bright and fresh, and well-lit from a landing window.

"Anyone home?" he called, and was startled when he heard an immediate response; footsteps above his head, in his bedroom—and Kate's.

"George, is that you?"

"Yes, m'dear. Just looked in for a cup of tea."

Kate's footsteps came clearly; he could picture her easy walk. Although she was getting rather heavy-breasted and thick at the waist, she was still graceful, and she didn't have to worry too much about her figure. She appeared at the head of the stairs, wearing a black skirt and a fresh white blouse, looking neat and wholesome; her hair was more grey than his, and she improved a natural wave deftly.

"You might as well shoot me as frighten me to death," she said. "I couldn't believe it was you when I heard the car, and when it drove off again——"

"Don't tell me you took any notice of a car pulling up outside!"

Kate had reached the foot of the stairs. With her broad forehead and high-bridged nose she was quite striking, and she used make-up well; more, these days, than she had a few years ago. Standing on the bottom stair, she was just an inch or two taller than he.

"Don't tell me you've just looked in for a cup of tea," she scoffed. "What did you leave behind?"

"Nothing, honest. I happened to be handy, and thought it would be a good idea to pop in."

"Crime *must* be in a bad way," Kate said.

It was only half serious, only half hurtful; in fact, hurtful was too strong a word. They had six children, the memory of a seventh, a certain kind of mutual dependence, and practically nothing else in common. In a queer way, one Gideon hadn't been aware of for a long time, he looked upon her as he might a stranger—Mrs. Lucy Saparelli, for instance.

"As a matter of fact," he said, "crime's flourishing. We've had a bad one to-day. Cleaned it up as well as it can be cleaned up, though."

"Oh." Kate moved, pushing past him, and their hands

brushed; hers was very cool. "Well, I don't suppose you've got long. Going to wait in the front room while I get it?"

"No, I'll come into the kitchen. Where's Malcolm?"

"Gone to the pictures with the Odlums," Kate said. "I think Mrs. Odlum knew all the others were out, and deliberately gave me an afternoon off. I was just going to do some window shopping."

They reached the kitchen. It was spick-and-span, and more than that. Kate knew what she wanted, and went all out to get it; and to help she had a little money of her own. That had always made a big difference to them. The kitchen was fresh and bright in pale blue and white paint, pale blue cake tins, pale blue handles on the saucepans. A new kitchen cabinet was painted the same colour—the carpentry and paintwork by Tom and Matthew Gideon! Everything had a clean smell. The gas popped. Gideon sat back in an old bed-chair, one of those Heath Robinson contraptions which could be turned into a bed to sleep an extra one, if needs be.

It was Kate's passion for tidiness, contrasting with his habit of coming home and littering the place, that had first really come between them; really contrast of temperaments. Funny thing, to think like that about the mother of your six— seven—children. One married a girl, loved, lived; after a while the intimacies became almost habitual, and since Malcolm's arrival——

The only time he'd known Kate hysterical was when she had known for certain that Malcolm was coming. In this very room she had cried and screamed and shaken her clenched fists at him.

"I won't have it, I won't have another brat. It's all I ever do! Work, slave, *breed*, work, slave and *breed*. And for you! What do you care? You're never in, never got five minutes to spare, and—I tell you I won't have it! I'll get rid of it somehow."

It had been a bad, even an ugly evening.

They had never really recovered from it, although oddly, she was passionately fond of Malcolm, and showed her affection more than she did with the others—showed it to Gideon that was; the children didn't know. If they did, it was because of some sixth sense that he knew nothing about.

"What kind of case was it?" asked Kate.

He sensed what she was feeling; as if this might be a chance to begin to get to know each other again. He'd made a gesture, she wanted to, too. She wasn't quite sure why he had come, and sitting back there and watching her, he wasn't sure either—except that one idea, which hadn't occurred to him before, came into his mind and wouldn't be dismissed. He had come home because he needed her; because the sight of little Dorothy Saparelli's mother had hurt him more than he knew.

The kettle was boiling.

Kate made the tea, and said, in a tighter voice: "Or is that a forbidden subject?"

"No," said Gideon. "No, Kate. Just nasty. A sex maniac, two little girls, and the hell that it's caused to a couple of families. I've just come from one of the mothers. It—well, you know what it is. Sometimes it makes me sick. Sometimes I wish I were one of the average crowd, lost in anonymity, doing a job which didn't make me rub shoulders with all the beastliness and the brutality there is. A man kills a child—and the pain goes on and on and on. By hanging him you don't make it any less. I'm not even sure that you don't make it more."

Kate was spooning sugar into his cup. The tea was very strong; sweet and strong, the way he liked it.

She took a big cake-tin out of the larder; the cake was already on a plate. Knives, plates and plastic mats appeared as if by sleight of hand.

"You look tired, George," she said abruptly.

"Oh, I'm all right."

"You can't give yourself a few hours off, I suppose?"

"Well—well, no, Kate. I wish I could."

She didn't answer.

The fruit cake was rich, too, and good; it had that richness of flavour that made each mouthful something to enjoy and to remember, not just to eat. He had another piece.

"Window shopping where?" he asked.

"Oh, in town! Knightsbridge or Oxford Street."

"How soon can you be ready?" asked Gideon. "I've got the car coming back in twenty minutes or so. Could give you a lift."

"Oh, that's lovely," Kate said in a flash. "All I need is five minutes. I must be back by half-past six, they'll start coming home soon after that—but it will give me a couple of hours to play truant in."

Then Gideon remembered Foster's sister, in Chelsea; he had meant to call on her on the way back to the Yard. The fact came to the tip of his tongue, but he didn't utter it. Kate looked suddenly gay. She was bright-eyed and eager, her grey hair didn't make her look her age. It wouldn't take him long to drop her, and then come back to Chelsea and Miss Foster—*Mrs. Addinson.*

"Thanks a lot, George, that was lovely," Kate said. "You must drop in more often!" Her eyes were bright with excitement, and she was laughing at him; with the children and with others—and at one time with him—she had always laughed easily. She didn't let him get out, but slammed the door and walked off, tall and brisk, something to see in her black suit and white hat and gloves. Gideon was in at the kerb, forgetful of the fact that he was in the way of Oxford Street traffic. He picked up the radio telephone.

Soon he was speaking to Lemaitre.

"Got something you want to see here, George—couple of good photographs of Foster, lying in the road." Lemaitre paused; a note in his voice suggested that he had something up his sleeve. "Going to be long?"

"Not long. Anything else?"

"Not to worry about. Sayer's made a clean breast of it, and the mystery of that kid in the tunnel out at Ealing isn't a mystery any longer. He did that, too. You know the job, three weeks ago. Haven't got a clue on that Islington killer, except that the chap was medium height and wore a brown suit. Used iron piping, and gloves—no dabs, not very optimistic." Lemaitre sucked his breath. "Half a mo'."

Gideon waited. Buses pulled up almost on the tail of his

car, and then swung out. Traffic filtered past, a constable
came up looking as if he had nothing in the world to do,
bent down, and peered at him.

"Going to be here long, sir?" He bumped his helmet on
the top of the window. "Oo!" Praiseworthy self-control.
"Holding up the traffic, you know, very bad place to stop."

"Yes. Sorry. Let me finish this talk to the Yard, and I'll
move off."

"To the——" There was a closer, sharper scrutiny. "I
didn't recognize you, sir! Sorry. Like me to make 'em give
you a bit more lee room?"

Gideon chuckled. "No, thanks, I'm all right."

The constable did his best to salute so that the courtesy
could be noticed, and moved off. There was the purr, the
hum, the roar of engines, the swish of wheels on the tacky
road, the perpetual motion of people weaving to and fro,
the air heavy with petrol fumes. Gideon eased his collar; his
neck was damp.

Lemaitre came again, almost bellowing:

"It's a flash from Waterloo. They've knocked off a van
with thirty thousand quid in it. One of our chaps caught a
packet. Three in one blasted day! Wonder if the others
were dummy jobs—be seeing you."

CHAPTER NINE

THE MAIL VAN JOB

A SMALL but well-set-up looking man in the early thirties, at the wheel of an Austin 10 saloon, cellulosed black, was drumming the steering wheel with the fingers of both hands, and watching a flow of traffic coming from the one-way street leading from Waterloo Road. Standing a few hundred yards away from him was another, younger man, dressed in drab grey and rather down at heel. He had a motor-cycle. Nearer the Austin was a short, stocky man who kept taking a cigarette out of his mouth, looking at it, then putting it back again.

All three had been there for ten minutes.

The stocky man near the Austin finished his cigarette, glanced up and down, and then stiffened; for a red mail van came in sight. It was on its own, clear of other traffic, and moving at a good speed.

The driver's hands stopped drumming. He started the engine. The others tensed, as if for action, although no one noticed them then.

The van didn't swing beneath the dark arches of the wide approach to Waterloo Station, but came straight on.

All three men relaxed; if relaxed was the word.

The stocky one came up to the car.

"You must have got it wrong."

The driver said smoothly: "I don't get things wrong."

"It's late, nearly ten minutes——"

"That's your watch, it's fast," the driver said. "Beat it, Ted."

"We can't stay around here any longer."

"What's the matter, losing your nerve? We'll stay as long as we have to. I got the squeak, didn't I? There are thirty thousand quid in that van, being sent down to Bournemouth."

"It'll have a cop tailing——"

"S'right," the driver said, "and we'll fix the cop and scram. Quit worrying. I'll see you at Shippy's, and——"

He stopped as another mail van came in sight. This time he didn't relax, for he read the registration number.

"That's it," he whispered, and the stocky man shot away from him as the Austin's engine started; then roared.

The Austin 10 was on the move as the van swung towards the archway; as it turned left, the Austin swung right. That was normal enough, for there was access to traffic from both directions.

Behind the van was a Wolseley with two men in it. Anyone who knew a Yard car would recognize that there was something unmistakable about the look of the man at the wheel and his companion. They weren't in any mood of alarm—until the man in drab grey, astride his motor-bicycle, roared alongside and tossed a little, fragile glass tube through the driving window. It broke on the driver's forehead. Ammonia gas billowed, biting at both Yard men's eyes, mouths and noses. The driver grabbed at the gear lever and his foot went down on the brake, but he was going fast and was blinded before he could stop. The police car lurched across and smashed into the archway wall. The man by the driver's side gave a funny little grunting sound as the door buckled and squashed him.

The car was slewed across the road; no other traffic could get in and it was a one-way stretch.

The Austin, a hundred yards further on, screeched alongside the mail van. The scarlet of the van's cellulose, bright under the sun, was reflected on the black shine of the car. The post office driver and his mate glanced sideways nervously, sensing what was happening. Brakes went on, but the Austin forced the van to keep on the inside, drawing just ahead of it. The Austin driver pulled a gun. The post office men didn't move.

Two youths, bent low until then and wearing black cloth masks, jumped from the back of the Austin. They didn't wait for keys, didn't speak, smashed at the padlock at the back of the little red van and, as the doors swung open, grabbed the registered bags—all of green canvas.

6

They rushed back to the Austin.

Within ninety seconds they were being driven away at furious but controlled pace, with the motor-cycle roaring after them. The post office men watched them go, and saw the registration plate of the saloon vanish. It had false plates; another would drop as soon as the robber car reached the Waterloo Road.

Back in the archway, cars were lined up behind the wreck. One Yard man was leaning against the wall, with tears still streaming down his face. Two men were pushing at the damaged car, so as to get at the driver's companion, who had slumped down in his seat; there was blood on his chin. Someone was calling for a doctor. Two uniformed policemen came hurrying.

The stocky youth, not needed to make a diversion after all, turned away and walked towards Whitehall, whistling.

Gideon switched off the radio-telephone and started his engine. He felt as if he were back where he had started; the all-pervading shadow of the mail van robberies had become blacker than ever. Whether the two earlier jobs had been to sell the police dummies or not, someone was bound to suggest that they had been, and two or three of the newspapers would have a smack at the Yard for it; and at him.

He was ten minutes' drive from the Yard.

He was fifteen minutes' drive from Foster's flat and his sister, Mrs. what-was-her-name?—Addinson.

"Can't prevent the damned hold-up now," he said aloud and savagely, "and if I don't see the woman soon I'll have to give the job to someone else."

He swung round in the road, where there was a clear stretch, nodded to the watching constable, and drove through Hyde Park towards the south-west and Chelsea.

It was then four o'clock.

Florence Addinson, née Foster, opened the door. At the first moment, she was just an attractive young woman, with features—expression?—a little too bold perhaps, wearing a washed-out blue smock daubed here and there with paint,

and poking red-lacquered fingers through her raven black
hair. Her hair was untidy and piled up on top with one of
those ring buns, or whatever they were called.

Then she recognized Gideon.

"Miss Foster," Gideon said, and felt irritated with himself; why use the wrong name when he knew it was
wrong?

"I—yes," she said, as if she didn't think it worth contra-
dicting him. "Yes, aren't you——"

"Superintendent Gideon."

"I thought you were." She hadn't moved away from the
door but held on to it tightly. Nervously? "Weren't you at
Mr. Chang's this morning?"

"Yes."

"Superintendent Gideon, can you tell me——" she began,
and then snatched her hand away from the door. "Oh, what
a fool I am! Won't you come in?"

"Thanks," said Gideon.

"I've just been doing some sketching," she said apolo-
getically. "A rush job."

"For Chang?"

"No, he—he changed his mind." She led the way into a
long, narrow room overlooking the Embankment.

Had Gideon ever entered this room during Foster's life, he
would soon have started wondering where the money came
from. Detective-sergeants didn't usually live in luxurious
apartments overlooking the Thames; or have dark, almost
black oak furniture, *circa* 1600, in a room which was richly
panelled and had several Dutch panels on the wall—each
worth something more than three figures.

Had they family money?

The woman stood and faced him and the impression that
she was nervous came back. She seemed younger than
Gideon had thought, partly because she'd not made-up since
morning, her cheeks had a scrubbed look. She no longer
looked over-bold, nor so attractive, if you liked smoothness
of line. The smock hid her figure, too, where her suit had
emphasized it.

Her eyes were almost black; like Foster's.

"Superintendent, is my brother in any trouble?" The question came out swiftly, quickened by embarrassment.

"What makes you think he might be?" asked Gideon.

"I—I don't know. That doesn't matter. Is he?"

"Yes, Miss Foster——" Gideon glanced down at her left hand; she wasn't wearing a wedding ring—"It would be pointless to lie to you, the papers have the story, I'm quite sure." He really meant that it would be a mistake to come out with all the truth now, but if he questioned her first and afterwards told her what had happened, what would she think of him?

What did it matter what she thought? He had a job to do.

"I'd like to know the truth." She was taut.

"Good. Do you mind telling me why you should think that he was in trouble?" When he chose to exert himself, Gideon could have the charm of a benevolent patriarch, and could inspire confidence even in people who ought to know better. "It might help a lot, in the long run."

She said abruptly: "He seemed worried."

"What about?"

"I don't know. I think——" she paused.

"I'll find out sooner or later, one way or the other," Gideon said, "and I've come myself because I thought it would help if you knew you were dealing with a senior officer."

"Oh," she said, and mechanically added: "Yes, thank you. Well, it's—it's hard to say. I think he was being threatened. He——"

Gideon's big hand now held the fat cigarette-case. Foster's sister took a cigarette. He lit it, then shepherded her to a window seat. It was rather a fine view, especially with the sun shining on the broad Thames, the two bridges in sight just far enough away to look fragile, and the plane trees lining the embankment powdered with light green; husks of the buds were beginning to litter the road and pavement.

The story came out swiftly.

The girl was no fool, and obviously had been worried for some time. At heart, she said, she'd been worried for two years, since Foster had first started to buy new furniture. Some of this was their own, which they'd inherited, but some pieces were recent acquisitions. All the paintings had been bought in the last year or so. He said he bought them at wholesale prices, and she had never voiced her anxiety to him.

Lately, she knew that he'd been worried; he hadn't slept much, he had been at work all day and out too much at night. She had felt sure that he was being put under some kind of pressure.

"Did you suspect anybody?" Gideon asked bluntly.

She didn't answer.

"Nothing you say to me will be used," Gideon said. "I might be able to switch inquiries, that's all. *Did* you suspect anyone?"

She said hesitantly: "Well—in a way. He—he knew that man Chang slightly, and I knew Chang had telephoned him. He always seemed more worried after that."

"Why did you go to Chang's?" Gideon asked.

"I—I thought I might find out something," she said. "Oh, I know it was silly, but I was really anxious. There'd been some talk of mural paintings for the new club-room, and I got an agency to introduce me to Chang about it. That's why I was there. I could have dropped through the floor when you arrived."

"You recognized me, didn't you?"

"You aren't a man to forget," she said.

Unexpectedly, that pleased him; she seemed to know that it did, and for a moment she was more relaxed. Then she changed and her voice hardened.

"What *has* happened? I've tried to get Eric on the telephone several times, but couldn't, and a sergeant I spoke to was most evasive."

"Hmm, yes," Gideon commented. He didn't like what he had to do, and the dislike stiffened his voice. "Rather ugly trouble, Mrs. Addinson. That's why I went to Chang's. I think Chang was bribing your brother to shut his eyes to certain offences."

She exclaimed: "Eric taking *bribes*?"

"Yes."

"You can't be certain!"

"No," agreed Gideon, "I can't really be certain."

"Where is Eric? What does he say?" She was flushed and very anxious.

"He denied it, of course," Gideon said, and went on very heavily: "Had you any reason to believe he was taking bribes?"

"No!"

Gideon thought: "I don't believe her." Then he began to wonder more about her; was her explanation of her visit to Chang the true one? Had she known Chang before? Was she involved? Were her present fears due to worry about the possibility of being caught out in some crime?

He saw her, now, just as another witness who might become a suspect. If Chang had warned her about Foster's danger from the Yard, it could explain much. The one thing that seemed certain was that she had not heard of the death of her brother.

"Mr. Gideon," Florence Addinson said abruptly, "will you please tell me where Eric is?"

"Yes," said Gideon, "although it's not a job I like, Mrs. Addinson. I hate bringing bad news of any kind." He felt that it had all gone wrong, he wasn't breaking this gently; she was expecting to hear that her brother was under arrest.

He must get it over.

"He was run down by a car this morning," he said, and stopped again.

He saw understanding dawning; surprise came first, because it was so unexpected, shock next; and the grief would come afterwards. He knew only too well that it was impossible to judge in advance how a woman would react to such news, but there was a one-in-four chance of a burst of hysteria. He let her have time to get used to the fear which he'd put into her mind, and then added quietly:

"It was over very quickly, I'm glad to say."

"*Over*," she ejaculated.

She sat on a cushioned window seat, back to the sun-gilt river, a few wisps of hair blowing slightly in the breeze from an open window. She didn't move. Sitting this way, the

smock was drawn down tightly; she had the kind of figure
Kate had had twenty years ago.

"*Over*," she repeated hoarsely.

"I'm afraid that's it," said Gideon, and liked the task less
than ever. "It's very distressing."

"I can't—I can't believe it!"

It was going to be hysteria. She'd jump up in a minute and
keep repeating that she couldn't believe it, and then she
would probably call it murder, and she would look round for
someone to blame. She was so young; middle twenties at
most, thought Gideon. Then he realized that he was letting
the emotional side gain the upper hand, he was seeing her as
an attractive woman. He had to see her as the sister of a
policeman who had accepted bribes, and probably had been
murdered; as a witness who might lead him to Chang and
beyond; to the distributors of drugs which corrupted and
killed.

She jumped up, hands clenched.

"It can't be true! Why, he left here this morning, as fit
as——"

She broke off.

Her colour was coming back, an angry red which seemed
to be reflected in her eyes.

Gideon watched her, not quite dispassionately.

He would let the first blast pass over his head, then try to
steady her, then he'd ring Lemaitre and have a couple of
good men come along here, to start searching. There had to
be a quick and thorough probe. She was on edge and likely
to remain so; if they could find one little pointer that involved her, they would be justified in trying to make her
crack. If she was in the clear, the sooner it was established
the better.

He watched her fighting for her self-control. Admiration
came back; it was impossible to rid himself of the curious
sense of personal concern for her.

Then she said: "I hope you'll tell me everything, Mr.
Gideon. Everything, please." She paused and then flung
out: "Did he kill himself?"

That startled Gideon.

"No," he said. "No, we've no reason to think so. Have you?"

"Just that he was worried. That man Chang. I——" she raised her hands and let them fall. "Anyhow, it's too late to do anything to help Eric now."

Very quietly, Gideon said: "You may be able to help us, Mrs. Addinson. Will you try?"

"In every way I can," she promised.

It was twenty to five when Gideon reached the Yard. He had waited there until Sergeants Wedderburn and Miller, the day's bright boys, had arrived at the flat. By then, Foster's sister had been completely composed, and he found doubts about her hard to retain. The two sergeants would go into figures, study all Foster's accounts, find out who the furniture was bought from, who sold Old Masters "at wholesale prices". It had all the makings of a nasty job, and Foster's game might have gone on for some time, but for Birdy.

Gideon had been thinking about the man who had really started his day. Birdy Merrick, at fifty-odd, had spent twenty years in jail. His was one of the worst records of any man in London for burglary and breaking and entering, but he had not been able to stand by and watch young girls become maddened with drugs. Good in every man? Certainly Birdy's love for his dead daughter had gone deep.

Gideon's office was empty.

He hung his hat with exemplary care on the peg in the corner, then took out his pipe and tobacco, next took off his coat, loosened his collar and, putting his right foot up on a chair, eased the lace of the shoe; the little toe was pinching a bit.

It was very warm. He sat down slowly, fingering the familiar roughness of his pipe and the smooth pouch at the same time, anticipating a smoke, feeling less tired than dispirited. That was partly due to Foster's sister. He thought of Kate asking him if he couldn't snatch a few hours off. It was so long since he had worked normal hours, and relaxed in the evening, that he had almost forgotten what it was like.

Lemaitre's hurriedly written notes were in front of him.

There was one about a patrolman's report on the painter at Chang's; a man known to have a chip on his shoulder, but as far as was known, quite honest; he'd never worked for Chang before, and Chang had tried three decorators before getting one who had been able to come at once. So the painter was out; Chang's anxiety to get the club painted quickly was more firmly in.

Another showed negative results from the inquiry about anyone with a "tough reputation" having left Chang's about eleven o'clock, and this confirmed, incidentally, that a decorating firm's foreman had been in to see Chang but had not been able to do an urgent job at the club. Chang, this report said, had wanted the decorating finished in time to open as usual that night.

The last report, at the bottom, made Gideon's teeth clench. Attached to it was a print of a photograph of Foster, lying dead in the road. He was face upwards. The photograph showed that the blood had oozed from his head into the dust of the roadway. It was a brilliant picture—a bit macabre, perhaps, if that were the word, but as a photograph vivid and clear in every detail. Obviously the car had crushed his stomach.

There was death looking at Gideon——

In the kerb was a dark patch and a shiny surface; a puddle. It had rained early morning. There was something else, and Lemaitre had pointed a red-pencilled arrow towards it. Gideon looked closer, and then his heart began to beat fast, he felt the choking throb of excitement.

The arrow pointed to a tyre track.

The tyre track looked familiar; and was familiar. It was of a new Michelin tyre, and the size was probably 5.50 x 16.

Lemaitre had written hurriedly:

"*Same make tyre as Gillick took a cast of, size and all, could be the same tyre, and if F. was bumped off by the mail v. boys—how about it?*"

CHAPTER TEN

FIND THAT TYRE

"THE only thing that matters," said Gideon to the Assistant Commissioner, who had come to his office, "is to find that tyre. It's one of the first real mistakes they've made, and they probably don't know it. If we can find that tyre——"

The A.C. was tall, lean, grey-haired, sardonic when the mood took him, and just now sardonically amused.

"All right, George. I want them as much as you do, but we needn't get excited about it."

"We needn't get——" began Gideon, explosively. He held his breath, then put his pipe down slowly. "If you were Lemaitre, I'd have your hide for that remark! I don't mind telling you that there's just one job——"

He broke off.

They looked at each other uncertainly and grinned simultaneously.

"Seem to have heard that before somewhere," said the A.C. "Where's Lemaitre?"

"Waterloo."

"He shouldn't have gone before you came back," said the A.C. mildly. "Drop him a hint that if he leaves the office empty I'll have *his* hide. I've just been looking through Sayer's statement. We've got a cold-blooded devil there."

Gideon didn't speak.

"And that Islington job, the old woman in the sweetshop," the Chief went on, "that's a bad one, too. Haven't had a chance to look at it much, have you?"

"No."

"More your cup of tea than anyone else's," the A.C. said, "and if it weren't, I've got to send Chatto to Portugal on that extradition job; he's the only one who can speak Portuguese well enough to get by in Lisbon, and I don't trust Portuguese

English. Smith's still up to his eyes in the City fraud case, I don't want to take him off. Deering's cracked up——"

"Deering isn't the only one near cracking up," Gideon said into a pause. "I'm all right, and will be for a bit, but flesh and blood is flesh and blood. We're all being driven too hard, from sergeants up. Had a chap with me to-day. Discovered he was on until two o'clock this morning, back on duty at six, and still at it. That's the way we make mistakes, and that's the way we'll go on making mistakes. Hasn't any blurry fool got any idea how to get our recruits' strength up?"

"No," said the A.C.

"I don't understand why it's so hard."

"Want your boys to become C.I.D. men?" asked the A.C. dryly. "Several years on the beat first at low pay with some danger, while there are plenty of good prospects elsewhere?"

"I wouldn't want my boys to become C.I.D. men if it made 'em millionaires," said Gideon forcefully. "Oh, I know what you mean, and I still think it's wrong recruiting methods. Bit more glamour, that's what we want. Well——" he broke off. "What brought you in, sir?"

It was a casual, belated "sir"; just as a matter of form.

"Islington," said the A.C. "Have a look at everything, will you, you've got X-ray eyes. And then there's the Moxley case. We don't want Moxley to get off, if ever a man deserved to be hanged he's the one. Sure the sergeant and the inspector you've briefed as witnesses are good enough?"

"As good as we'll get," Gideon assured him. "But don't count on a verdict. Moxley killed his wife all right, and he did it because of that tart who gets her face and fanny plastered all over the papers, but it's going to be tough. Not a thing more we can do about it, either. That rape job's up in Number 2 at the Old Bailey in the morning, too. We'll get those little baskets all right. Cor!"

The A.C. said: "Seamy, isn't it?"

"What I want is to get away, have a nice clean breeze running through my hair for a bit," said Gideon, "but it won't be for a few months yet. I—excuse me."

The telephone bell rang. He picked it up, sitting on a corner of the desk. The A.C., a tailor's dummy of a soldier in mufti, stood waiting. Gideon's expression told him nothing, Gideon's voice told him a lot.

"Hallo, Birdy," said Gideon.

He listened . . .

"All right," he said, "I'll send it over to you in old notes . . . I don't know, but someone who'll recognize you. Then lie low for a bit, don't get yourself into trouble. . . . Unless you tell me anything more about Chang."

He paused.

"Okay, Birdy," he said and rang off.

He rubbed his hand across his forehead; both hand and forehead were damp.

"That's the squeaker on Chang and Foster, sir." Here, if ever, was a time for formality. "I'm paying him twenty-five pounds and it's cheap at the price. Two men are over at Foster's place now, I hope to have some kind of a report before I go off to-night." He sniffed. "Birdy says that there's a call out for him and he wants to get away." Suddenly the two men, broadsword and rapier in contrast, were standing upright and looking squarely at each other; each with genuine respect. "I don't like it, A.C. Foster was probably run down deliberately because once we found out what he was up to, he might have squealed."

"But Chang——"

"Don't want to make it worse than it is," said Gideon, "but why assume that Chang was the only one he was taking bribes from? I don't say he wasn't, yet I can't see Chang paying out a fortune, and somehow Foster's cashed in pretty big money. Did you know that the tyre mark near Foster's body might match up with the one at Battersea? —the car from which they threw those mailbags into the river."

The A.C. said, "No, I didn't."

"Come'n have a look." They pored over the photographs, Gideon's flat but well-shaped and clearly marked forefinger pointing at similarities. "And that blakey settles it," he said. "See where it's embedded in the tyre—comes out in the cast

and in the photograph clearly under magnification. Look."
He thrust a round magnifying glass into the A.C.'s hand.

The A.C. pursed his lips.

". . . mmm. I see what you mean. Well, I'll finish off
where I came in—Find that Tyre!"

He went out.

Gideon wrote out a chit for twenty-five pounds. He
charged it to the Information Account, rang for a plainclothes officer, and sent him along to cash it. When the man
came back, Gideon was staring at the ceiling, and actually
smoking; he owed himself an extra pipe, had only had one
that morning.

"Thanks. Green, do you know Birdy Merrick?"

"Oh, yes, sir."

"Sure?"

"Little chap with a chirruping voice and a little beak of a
nose that's always red. Been inside——"

"That's the chap. Take this over to him—he'll be near the
telephone kiosks at Aldgate Station by the time you get there.
Don't let him put his hands on it until you've got his signa-
ture on the receipt. I like Birdy, but you can guess how far
I'd trust him."

Green, delighted at a chance to go out, chuckled with more
than polite amusement.

When he'd gone, Gideon sat and pulled at his pipe and
looked at a spot on the ceiling. It had been there for five
years and he still didn't know how it had got there; a pale
brownish spot about the size of half a crown. In it, he had
seen many things and many faces. Leaning back in the
swivel chair with the strong spring back at just the right angle,
he could see it with complete comfort. He'd trained himself
to lean back like this, a form of relaxation that was almost
complete. In a minute, he would treat himself to a double
whisky, then he would be set for a few hours.

He thought of Kate.

He thought of Foster's sister.

He had his whisky.

He thought of Lucy Saparelli. Those kids. Sayer. A little
old woman with a battered head.

This was one of the bad days, but the newspapers would look much the same as usual next morning; half the headlines in the popular daily press were about major crimes. No one would be surprised. Now and again there was an outcry about unsolved crimes, and so there should be. Only one crime in two, not even as many as that some years, were ever solved. The miracle was that the Yard got so many results. Give them a ten per cent. increase in staff——

The door opened, and Lemaitre came in, brand new trilby on and slightly at the back of his head, perky of feature and expression, grinning rather smugly.

"Hi!" he greeted.

"When you're going to leave the office empty again, make sure that the Old Man isn't coming in, will you?" Gideon said flatly.

Lemaitre's perkiness vanished; he positively sagged.

"You don't mean to say——"

"I do mean to say, and why you ask for trouble like that I don't know. Rule Number 1—always have someone in the office. If we both *have* to be out, fetch in a sergeant." Gideon grinned. "But it's up to the Old Man to discipline you, you rebellious old so-and-so. Got anything from Waterloo?"

Lemaitre began to look less disconsolate. He took his hat off and twirled it round his forefinger, formed his mouth into a soundless whistle, and then said:

"Yes."

That thumping started again at Gideon's chest.

"What?"

"Tyretrack, believe it or not. Patch of oil on the approach to the station, just where the van was held up. A lorry had a puncture there a few nights ago, and dripped a lot of engine oil. The rain had smoothed it out. One track as clear as a cucumber, unmistakable, too—but if I hadn't gone there it wouldn't have been noticed. All the photographs they took before I arrived were of the mail van. Five minutes more and they'd have trampled all over the oil patch. Now tell the Old Man——"

"No one said you shouldn't go out on a job sometimes, just

be your age and make sure someone's here," said Gideon. He had the patience of a schoolmaster with Lemaitre, who had one thing which no one else at the Yard had quite so well developed: a "natural" sense of observation. Lemaitre's eyes did most of his work for him; he'd miss nothing out, and he could check another man's case brilliantly. If he could only restrain his impetuosity, he'd be a genius. "So, what have we got?" Gideon asked.

"Three Michelin tyre tracks," Lemaitre said. "One near Chang's—one at Battersea—the third at Waterloo. I know, I know, three different cars could——"

"They probably didn't. Anything else?"

"It was an Austin 10 with false number plates. The driver had black hair, and his cap was pulled low over his eyes, showing his hair from the crown downwards. *And*," went on Lemaitre, voice rising in triumph, "one of those post office johnnies kept his eyes open although he admits he was scared stiff. The black hair had a white mark in it—scar of some kind, starting just level with the right ear. Now we can look for the car, the tyre and the driver, and oh, boy——"

He broke off because a telephone bell rang on Gideon's desk.

"Yes," said Gideon into it, and then repeated, although looking puzzled: "Yes, put him through." He glanced up at Lemaitre. "It's Green, chap I sent to pay Birdy his blood money. Move your big head, I can't see the clock." Lemaitre moved quickly. "H'm. Five and twenty past six. Been gone twenty minutes." He waited with the receiver at his ear. Then: "Yes, Green?"

He listened.

He began to look very grim indeed.

"All right," he said at last, "stay there another twenty minutes, and if he hasn't turned up then, come back. 'Bye."

Gideon rang off, scowled, looked at Lemaitre steadily, and said flatly: "Someone sent a kid to tell Green we wouldn't be able to pay Birdy off to-night or any night. I don't like that at all." He lifted the telephone, a mechanical action. "Give me G5 headquarters," he said, and added for Lemaitre's benefit, although he sounded as if he was talking to himself: "Better get the Division to keep an eye open for him."

"We can't afford to lose Birdy," Lemaitre said, and meant it.

CHAPTER ELEVEN

BIRDY

"BIRDY," Birdy's wife said, "they're after you."

"Wife" was not strictly true, in the legal sense, but in all others it was. She was a small, faded woman, who had never been pretty, was balloon-breasted now, but still had small if work-torn hands—the fingers of her right hand were especially rough, for she was a seamstress. She also had beautifully shaped legs and feet. In spite of her weight and her top-heavy look, she moved very easily.

She had caught up with Birdy at the telephone boxes in the approach to Aldgate Station. The traffic in the wide main road was a hurtling, hooting mass, choking the golden evening. Barrow boys with fruit stalls magnificently arranged shouted whether customers were near or not, newsboys droned. This great mouth of London's East End and the suburbia beyond throbbed with a vitality which it saw only once each day, always between half-past five and half-past six. All London seemed to be on the move.

Policemen walked; plodding, watchful, patient.

Thieves watched for their chances.

Pickpockets made theirs.

It isn't even remotely true that everyone in the East End, from Wapping to Rotherhithe, or from Bethnal Green to Whitechapel, is a criminal, or even criminally inclined. But ask any London policeman where crime and criminals flourish most, and he will unhesitatingly point to this part of the city. A few might say that at times there was a greater concentration of vice in the West End Square Mile, but very few are sure.

Most of this East End trouble area came within the jurisdiction of G5 Division. The Division had picked officers and picked men, and knew its job inside out. Like every other section of the London police it was understaffed, but it was more generously treated than most.

Every policeman in the Division knew Birdy, and most of them knew Birdy's "wife". An odd thing about Birdy was that he looked small, mean, sneaky and nasty altogether, yet he wasn't. He had a kind of morality. He had a kind of courage. He acted upon a kind of code. Take Birdy and his "wife"—her name was Ethel—out of the slums where they lived and worked, out of the tiny, smelly hovel with its front door opening on to the pavement, put them in one of the clean sweet-smelling suburbs, and Birdy might be heard to say that his wife was the best woman in the world, and Ethel would certainly be heard to say that they didn't come any better than her Birdy.

He had a slightly hunched back, and was sparrow-thin, but very bright with a Cockney twang and a Cockney's swift repartee.

Now, he looked into Ethel's scared eyes.

" 'Ow'd you know?" he asked and caught his breath.

"Murphy's been around," she said. "Someone told me at Shippy's, so I went 'ome. 'E come to see me, wanted to know where to find you."

"Murphy," echoed Birdy, and licked his lips.

"Syd's at one corner, Hicky at another," Ethel went on, "waiting for you."

"Syd," echoed Birdy, "and——" he didn't repeat "Hicky".

"Any—any of the kids in?"

"Dunno."

"Look here," said Birdy, and licked his lips again, "we got to make sure they don't 'urt the kids. You better go rahnd to the Pie Shop, or git Dais to go, or telephone, see."

"Okay, but what about you?"

Birdy said: "I'll be okay." He twisted his lips into a smile that called for a lot of courage, and did nothing to betray the suffocating fear which made his heart beat with a kind of sluggish reluctance. "I'll lie low fer a bit, don'chew worry."

"But Birdy——" Ethel looked, felt and sounded anguished.

"You look arter yourself," Birdy urged, "and leave me to look arter myself, Ethel. Scram, ducky." He gave her a slap, then turned away from the surging, growling traffic towards the bowels of the earth and the Underground that swallowed London's millions, gestated, and then spewed them up. A train was roaring down below. It stopped. A great surge of people, all eyes blinking, came up the wide stairs towards the welcoming light. Birdy was pressed against the wall, close to a colourful tobacco kiosk, where a shiny-haired woman began to serve as fast as she could.

Then the crowd passed and for a moment there was calm.

Birdy had only one idea; to get away from here. There was no safety in the East End. There was little safety anywhere, once "they" came after him, or after anyone. He knew, because he had been on the run once before, and it had lasted for several weeks—until the police had cleaned up the gang that had come for him.

Now, he fingered the scar beneath his right eye; a vitriol scar. He still didn't know what had saved him from being blinded.

He reached the top of the stairs. A man wearing a purple choker, a lightweight, American-style coat with big stains on the wide lapels, was at the foot, grinning up at him. In the distance, another train rumbled.

Birdy missed a step when he saw the man. He did not reason, because panic came too close. The only sound he could hear now was the banging of his heart; painful, frightening. This meant that "they" were out in strength. The Murphy Gang was the strongest in London at the moment, twenty or thirty strong. Like all the successful gangs, and those which flourished at all, it restricted its activities, worked mostly within the G5 boundary, and operated mostly against rival crooks. It had cannibal instincts. Its members were brutish, sadistic and utterly without scruple. It wasn't a gang in the sense that it had headquarters or acted in concert, but only in that it accepted Murphy's leadership. He got the jobs, paid the men off, gave them protection; he would hide them, get them alibis, do anything that was necessary to keep them safe from the

law—and he would get his man. Now he had been given a
job, and Birdy thought he knew who had given it to him.

Chang.

The job was simply to "get" Birdy.

Birdy knew nothing at all beyond that. It might mean to
kill him; it might mean to maim him; it might mean to torture
him. There was no end to what it might mean, and that was
one of the worst fears: the uncertainty. Only two weeks ago,
"they'd" gone after that poor little cove, Charlie Lin. Lin,
half Chinese, half Cockney, was runner for a fence, and had
kept more than his share of payment for a job. He had
probably been cheated for years and driven to desperation,
running the risks of taking money to the thief and the hot
goods to the fence. He'd kept back a fiver, and the fence had
hired Murphy.

One part of Birdy's mind told him that the fence wouldn't
have done that if a fiver had been the only thing at stake.
More likely, the fence was frightened in case Lin squealed.

Lin was in hospital being well looked-after. At least he
wasn't frightened any more. They'd amputated his right leg
and the fingers of his left hand, and there was some doubt
whether he would ever be able to see again. He'd been found
in a battered heap in a rubber warehouse, and there was no
trace of the brutes who had done it, although the East End—
including G5 Division—knew that it had been a Murphy
job.

Murphy hadn't laid a hand on Lin.

No one knew who had—for Murphy would have given the
order to four or five of the boys, who wouldn't talk except
among themselves. One might have a drink too many and
say what he shouldn't, but that didn't happen very often.
Usually orders were given at a café in the Mile End Road—a
place called Shippy's, after its owner, whose name was
Shipham.

"Shippy's" was a byword.

Well, there was Lin . . .

There was the swaggering man with the broad grin at the
foot of the steps.

Birdy turned away as a train rumbled in, another one from

the West End. This would disgorge its hundreds, too. He hurried to get out of the station first and then saw Ali.

Ali was a lascar.

No one knew when Ali had last been aboard ship, and it didn't matter. He was a little Indian who spoke broken English, had smooth, dark skin, beautiful black eyes and beautiful, shiny black hair; a model for any painter. No one quite knew what went on in his mind, no one quite knew what he did with his days, but they knew him for a remarkably able knife artist. Ali could carve patterns on cheek or belly, arm or breast. He was lounging against the telephone kiosk, with his right hand in his pocket.

He was right-handed.

Birdy missed a step.

A policeman, big and genial, and hot in thick serge, came along, saw Ali, and lost his smile. Ali had never been inside and had never had his prints taken, and it was the oath of every man on the beat in the Division to get him. Ali stared back at the policeman. He didn't smile, either, but looked with an unmistakable impudence which could make a level-headed policeman lose his temper. The temptation to break Ali's neck was sometimes overpowering.

The train roared into the station.

Birdy waited. The policeman walked on, but took up a position, as if Ali's expression warned him of impending trouble and he meant to stop it. Then the crowd surged up the steps, caught up with Birdy and swept him out of the wide open mouth and past Ali. He caught a glimpse of Ali trying to breast the tide of humanity and keep level, but pilgrims bathing in the Holy Water of the Ganges could not have kept him away more successfully.

Birdy nipped across the road.

No member of Murphy's gang was in sight, as far as he could judge, but he didn't know all of Murphy's gang; no one did. That was another of the factors which made it unspeakable horror to be hunted by the gang. Birdy could go to the police and ask for protection, and he would get it for a while; only for a while. Once he did that he would cut off all hope for the future. The whole of the fraternity would turn against him, against Ethel and against the kids. They knew he squeaked sometimes, but they also knew that he squeaked only about dope, and that his daughter, by his first and real wife, had been an addict. They didn't blame Birdy for what he did, but if he stepped outside that one form of squeaking, they'd turn on him.

If he couldn't look after himself, they'd have no time for him either.

He was in this on his own and the heat was on. His hope was to get somewhere to lie low until it was off. The police might get Chang, and if Chang couldn't pay Murphy, Murphy wouldn't be interested. It was a matter of time.

Birdy turned down a narrow street leading towards Tower Hill. The East End was too hot for him, his best chance was down in the city, in one of the warehouses. One could live there for days, for weeks, without being seen, emerging only after dark, feeding at one of the little coffee stalls at Billingsgate. It would be dark in an hour and a half, if he could stay safe until after dark he would be all right.

There was another serious worry: Ethel.

Birdy was sweating.

Murphy would know that he wouldn't tell Ethel where he was going, wouldn't he? Murphy was bad, Murphy's gang didn't care whether they worked on a man or a woman, but they didn't waste their time. They'd be sure that he, Birdy, hadn't confided in Ethel——

Wouldn't they?

He reached the end of a narrow road which led to Tower Hill, and saw Lefty.

Lefty was a snowy-haired youth of nineteen, who looked cherubic enough for Leonardo. His strength was the broken beer bottle, thrust into a man's face and twisted. He was one of Murphy's gang.

Had he heard about the hunt for Birdy?

Birdy nipped back into a doorway, but didn't go fast enough. Lefty didn't smile, didn't change his expression, just sauntered towards Birdy. He wore a big, baggy, black jacket and there was a bulge, the kind of bulge likely to be made by a beer bottle with the neck smashed off. This was in his left-hand pocket. He was called Lefty for the obvious reason.

Birdy turned and ran.

Lefty didn't run; he whistled softly. It was only a matter of time.

Gideon looked at the clock; it was just after six. He yawned, but it was much too early to start yawning. This was a day which might last its full twenty-four hours. He knew himself well; what he needed now was a good meal, well-cooked vegetables and some good red meat, a pint of beer and forty winks. Once he'd put that inside him he would be all right, but he might not have time.

Lemaitre was out again.

The telephone bell rang.

"Gideon," said Gideon. "Oh, hallo, Fred, what's on?"

He listened, turned down his lips, made one or two notes, muttered an unenthusiastic thanks, and put the receiver down. He began to doodle on a blotting pad, and after a couple of minutes told himself that it was further evidence of the fact that he was running down and needed replenishing.

Lemaitre came in.

"George," he said, as a man with a worry, "I've just been downstairs to see my missus. Remember, I'm a married man? I forgot that I told her we'd go along for a snack to the Troc, and blow me, she's got tickets for the Arthur Askey show. If I can't go, *you've* got to tell her." His anxiety was comical.

Gideon said: "How long've you got?"

"She's come with the handcuffs," Lemaitre said.

"About the only way they'll ever drag us away," Gideon grunted. "Wouldn't be a bad idea if we laid on a campaign. Now if Kate——" he drove the fanciful thought off. "Okay, Lem, I don't know that there's anything to keep you." What he did know was that this would keep him here until the small hours. "Just had a word with Fred Hartley."

" 'Bout Birdy?"

"Yes. The Murphy gang's out."

Lemaitre said: "Oh, gawd! Poor tick's had it now."

"One day we'll get round to Murphy," Gideon said. "Anyway, Birdy's on the run. We're all looking out for him, and if our chaps find him first they'll pull him in on a charge. Not that Birdy'll want that. Still . . ." Gideon stood up, slowly. He felt very hungry, the kind of raw emptiness that affected one's nerves and muscles, made one sag, started the tight feeling at the back of the eyes. "And Fred's worried about Birdy's woman and the two kids. So he's tipped off Black Jo, and Jo's looking after the family. Murphy won't risk a gang fight, I shouldn't think, but Black Jo won't lift a finger to help Birdy, although he'll help the woman. High Life in Civilized London!" He scratched his chin. "Send for a sergeant, Lem, and then sort everything out so that it's in apple-pie order when I get back."

"Okay. Where you going?"

"Across to the pub to get a square meal, and I'll tell Fifi about her good luck on the way."

He was smiling when he went outside; he always smiled when he thought of Lemaitre's wife as Fifi, which was her real name. A French grandmother's influence—or was it grandfather? Skittish little blonde, no better than she ought to be, but then, Lem Lemaitre wasn't exactly a one-woman man. The frailty of human nature——

Fifi was in the main hall and there was an exceptionally good-looking constable on duty there. She was overdressed in a plum-coloured suit and a cherry-and-plum hat, and didn't look bored. Gideon told her Lem would be down in a few minutes, and then walked across the yard towards Cannon Row and the convenient pub where he knew he could get a meal that any trencherman would enjoy. He could afford to relax for half an hour or so, too. It was easy to forget that the Yard didn't stop working, whatever he or anyone else did. Thousands of coppers were on the look-out for that Austin with a Michelin tyre, and there was just a chance that they'd have some luck to-night.

Odd thing, that tyre.

He thought about it a lot during the meal—roast saddle of mutton, mint sauce and new potatoes, with rich, fatty gravy —probably the potatoes came out of a tin, but they had the true Jersey flavour. He ploughed steadily through the meal, refusing to be hurried, making it clear that he didn't want to talk to the other Yard men, the reporters and a couple of sergeants from Cannon Row Police Station who were at the bar.

Chang—Foster—the Battersea riverside—the Waterloo Station job. If it were the same tyre, and there wasn't much doubt, this could really lead to something big. But it connected Chang with some of the post office robberies, and that was a very nasty possibility. The worst thing about the mail van jobs were the tips that the robbers had in advance. They always knew when a van would have a valuable load on, they knew when it would leave one place and was due at another; and of late, Yard men on duty at key points had been attacked and prevented from going to the rescue. Today's two morning jobs had suggested a break in the system, but now——

Had Foster been one source of the leakage?

Foster wouldn't have known anything about the Waterloo job, would he?

The door opened, and King-Hadden, the Superintendent of *Fingerprints*, came in. If Gideon had a close friend at the Yard, as apart from a mass of good friends with mutual liking, it was King-Hadden. This man had succeeded one of the most brilliant fingerprint men the Yard had ever had, and he wasn't doing so badly. In fact, what King-Hadden didn't know about prints no one knew. He was a world authority, and in the middle-forties; he couldn't get any higher.

"Hallo, George."

"Come and sit down, Nick."

"Thanks." The barmaid's help hovered. "Bessie— double whisky and not too much soda, please." He dropped down into a chair opposite Gideon. "Got some good news for you, chum," he said.

"Wassat?" Gideon's mouth was full of succulent roast potato, oozing fat.

King-Hadden grinned as he took a small envelope from his inside breast pocket. He was a big, plump, pale, rather shapeless man, whose intelligent eyes usually held a laugh. Coins chinked in the envelope. He opened it, and let three sixpences roll out on to the cloth; two of them were stained slightly, as if with brown wax.

Gideon knew a dried bloodstain when he saw it.

"Prints on two," said King-Hadden, "middle of the thumb, right index finger—could be the left. It depends on what pocket he had the money in."

"Who and what money?"

"The Islington shop job."

Gideon said sharply: "No!"

"Yes. This was found on the pavement at a bus stop this afternoon. The kid who saw it was being watched by a copper. He recognized bloodstains. They fell out of the pocket of a man dressed in a brown suit, who was waiting for a bus at Islington Town Hall. That's five minutes' walk away from the shop where the old woman was killed. About the time of the job, too. The copper kept his wits about him, lot of good to be said for training some of the uniformed boys in C.I.D. work, whatever there is against it. He turned them into the Division."

Gideon said: "Any record?" as if it were too much to hope.

"Oh, yes," said King-Hadden blandly, "didn't I tell you?" He looked smug and his eyes glistened. "Identified them as the prints of Arthur George Fessell, who's been inside twice for robbery with violence. The call's gone out for him. See—all we do is your work, while you sit gluttonizing!" He glanced up. "Ta, Bessie, I'll drink your health." He picked up a whisky and soda, sniffed it, and sipped. "Ah, I needed that. Going home?"

"To-morrow, maybe!"

"Well, I'm off now," said King-Hadden, "I keep my department up to date. Cheers. By the way, there's another little thing that may amuse you. They've picked up that Austin with the Michelin tyre you've been making such a fuss about. Parked in Haymarket. Lemaitre's over there, waiting until the driver turns up for it, and his Fifi's giving him merry hell. Cheers," King-Hadden repeated, and sipped again.

Bessie, flat-breasted and big-handed, approached them again.

"Want any sweet, Mr. Gideon?"

Gideon was rubbing his hands together and looking as pleased as a prizewinner schoolboy.

"I do, Bessie," he said. "Treacle pudding's on, isn't it? Plenty of treacle, remember. And after that a bit of Dorset Blue and some butter. This isn't such a bad day after all," he confided in King-Hadden. "We got Sayer, we've got a line on the Islington chap, Fessell you say? and now this tyre—not at *all* a bad day. Let me buy you a drink."

"One's enough before I drive to the danger of the public," said the flabby man. "How's Kate?"

"Fine!"

"Must have a Sunday together again when the weather gets a bit better," said King-Hadden. "Might make it this week-end if it keeps like to-day. Meg'd like it. Well, good luck, hope you catch 'em all, but don't forget the day's only just started!" He sipped again. "Be a funny thing if we could sit back now and know in advance what's going to happen to-night, wouldn't it? What's sure to happen? A dozen burglaries, a murder, dopies getting dopier, girls being laid for the first time, someone sitting back and plotting a coup for to-morrow, someone getting rid of the thirty thousand quid they picked up at Waterloo—who'd be a copper?" He finished his drink. "So long, George."

He went out.

Two minutes later Birdy's wife came in.

CHAPTER TWELVE

TWO TALES OF JEWELLERY

GIDEON recognized Ethel Merrick on the instant, long before she saw him. He judged from the expression on the faces of some of the other men that they also recognized her. She stood there, wearing a grey suit and a white blouse, a huge, frilly blouse which was stretched so tightly that it looked as if someone had stuffed it as sausage meat or sage and onions in a turkey. She had on a coat that was too small for her and strained open at the front. Her small red hat had a blue feather broken at the tip and her patent leather shoes had very high heels. No one could fail to see her distress, no one could miss the graceful shapeliness of those calves and ankles.

Then she saw Gideon, opened her mouth, gulped, and walked towards him.

He stood up.

No one else watched now.

"Hallo, Mrs. Merrick," Gideon said, "come and sit down."

He could hear her agitated, bubbly breathing, almost as if she were asthmatic. She was pale, her forehead and upper lip were wet with sweat. Gideon pulled out a chair, and she licked her lips as she sat down, and then eased her coat under the right arm. Bessie, who had a wonderful sense of timing, appeared with the treacle pudding.

"What will you have, Mrs. Merrick?" asked Gideon.

"Oo, thanks ever so!" Ethel caught her breath. "Could I —could I 'ave a gin and It, I need to buck meself up a bit."

"Of course you can. Double gin and a splash of Italian, Bessie," said Gideon. "Cigarette, Mrs. Merrick?" The big case, with one side filled with cigarettes, the other half empty, was held out in front of her.

"Ta," she breathed, and when she had settled down, added gustily: "It's ever so good of you to make me feel at home like this, Mr. Gideon, I wouldn't have come if I wasn't so worried about Birdy." Then her fear affected her words. "They—they're *arter* him."

Gideon said calmly: "Who is, d'you know?"

"Why, Murphy's gang! Mr. Gideon, I know Birdy's done a lot of criminal things, but—oo, *ta*, dearie." She almost snatched the glass out of Bessie's hand, for Bessie also had a trick of speed when it was necessary, and gulped. "Oo, that's better. But he's not bad like some people, like that Murphy for instance. He——"

"Has Murphy threatened you?" asked Gideon hopefully.

"Well, no, not in so many words, but that don't count, do it? He come and asked where Birdy was, said he just had to see him, that's enough for me. Mr. Gideon, can't you pull Birdy in?"

"He's got a clean sheet these past few weeks, Mrs. Merrick."

"Oh," said Ethel Merrick, "'e 'as, 'as 'e?" She had given up the struggle with aspirates. "Well, it's not that I like squealing on me own ole man, but don'chew believe it. Remember the Marshall Street jeweller's job? That was Birdy! Got some of the rings at home now, 'e—'e 'id them," she added hastily. "I come across them by accident. Ain't that enough, Mr. Gideon?"

It was plenty.

She knew that if she appealed for police help against Murphy, it would do Birdy a lot of harm. She knew that she dared not go to the Division, because it would be reported. She also knew that if the police wanted Birdy for a "job" it would be a different matter. He would get at least three years if he were sent down for the Marshall Street robbery, and she thought it worth sending him down; that was a measure of her fear.

Gideon didn't want Birdy inside, but he'd have to put him there.

"All right, Mrs. Merrick," he said, "I'll do what I can. We knew that Birdy was in trouble and we're looking out for him. Don't worry too much. This'll have to be done from the local station, you know that——"

"So long as you'll fix it," Ethel pleaded.

Gideon went across to the Yard and "fixed it".

There was no news of Birdy. There was no further word from Lemaitre. Fifi was probably on her way to the theatre by herself, now—Gideon hoped she would not pick up a "friend". The only man at the Yard who didn't know most of what there was to know about Fifi was Lemaitre.

Gideon forgot that.

There was the fingerprint job that King-Hadden had done, and now that he saw photographs of the coins, enlarged to ten times their real size, he was able to marvel at the efficiency of King-Hadden's work; the fragment of the fingerprint on the bloodstained coins was so fractional that few men would have tried to identify it. With luck, it would hang Fessell, whose dossier was on Gideon's desk. It made ugly reading.

Gideon began to wonder wryly about King-Hadden's airy talk of the day "just beginning".

Dusk was falling, the day's brightness had quite gone, there were lights at some of the windows across the court-yards, and he could see lights on the cars and buses which passed along Parliament Street; he could see a few yards of the street from the window, too.

What was certain to happen? King-Hadden had asked.

Burglary; robbery with violence; murder—no, it wasn't as bad as that yet, murder was certain once or twice a week, but not once a day. There was the whole range of crimes, from major to minor. At this moment men were getting themselves into the toils of women who would never let go, blackmail was being nurtured, frightened people were blustering, there were young girls, perhaps completely innocent girls like Penelope, girls much younger than Pru, smoking their first reefer, feeling a terrific excitement and a tremendous kick and not knowing that they were on the way down to hell upon earth.

Somewhere men and women were out at dinner or at the pictures, who would go home and find their houses burgled. People were sitting at their own table at this very moment, not knowing that a thief had broken in and was even now raiding the woman's bedroom above their heads. It was a never-ending cycle. Gideon's one hope was that whatever happened, it would happen in such a way that he did not have to tackle anything new to-night.

His telephone rang.

"Gideon."

"There's a Mrs. Addinson here, sir," the hall sergeant told him. "She would be glad if you could spare her a few minutes."

Foster's sister had made up, and dressed for effect. Black suited her, the white blouse and cuffs gave a touch of purity. Nice-looking, wholesome woman. Only her eyes hinted at strain, and this eased when Gideon made her welcome and gave her a cigarette. No two women could contrast more sharply than Florence Addinson and Birdy's "wife".

"What can I do for you, Mrs. Addinson?" Gideon was almost casual.

"I've come because I think I can help you," she said.

Gideon didn't show how that quickened his pulse.

"That's good. How?"

"I've been going over everything that Eric's been doing and saying," she said. "We had a—a quarrel a night or two ago, because he was never in. He used to pretend he was always on duty, but I knew he wasn't. I said so, and—and he flared up."

"I see," Gideon said. He did not intend to help her; just to let it come. There was still the possibility that she was involved, even though her visit made that seem less likely.

"You may not think so, but I really want to help," she said, a little sharply. "I'm reconciled to the fact that Eric was—was doing wrong. I'd like to think that whoever made him do it suffers, too."

Gideon relaxed.

"You don't want that any more than we do." He looked almost eager. "Really think you can help?"

"I'm not sure, but something he said might give you something to go on—unless you *know* who bribed him." She added that so quickly and unexpectedly that it was possible to believe that it was the focal point of her visit; that she had really come to try to find out how much he knew.

Would Chang, would anyone, venture such tactics?

Gideon just couldn't be sure.

"We guess a lot," he said, and left it at that. "What was it that your brother said?"

"He was really talking to himself," Foster's sister answered. "As he was going out of the room, he said: 'I'd be a damned sight better off living with Estelle.' I didn't know whom he meant, I'd never heard him talk of a girl named Estelle. But a woman of that name telephoned me this evening."

Now she really sparked Gideon's interest.

"Oh? What about? Eric?"

"Yes," Foster's sister said wryly. "She said that Eric had been murdered. She sounded quite hysterical, and rang off before I could get any more sense out of her." Flo Addinson paused, eyeing Gideon very intently, before she went on: "Was Eric murdered?"

Gideon answered bluntly: "It's just possible."

After a pause, Foster's sister said quietly: "Thank you. I thought you might look for this woman, Estelle."

"Believe me, we'll look for her," Gideon promised. "You've given us a lead which might be invaluable. If there's anything else——"

"There's just one thing," she said. "I'd like to help actively, and I think I might be able to."

Now, he was wary. "How, Mrs. Addinson?"

"I could harass Chang," she said. "There's a picture of a dancer outside his office, and her name's Estelle. It could be the same one." How Lemaitre would benefit from some of her caution! "I thought if I went to see Chang, asked him about what really happened, asked about Eric and Estelle——"

"No," Gideon was abrupt, "leave Estelle right out of it, you'd only warn Chang that we were interested in her. I'll check the dancer, though, that's most useful."

He stopped.

"May I try to harass Chang?" she asked, and then added very quickly, almost fiercely: "I don't think anything could keep me away, but if—if you could suggest how to handle him——"

Gideon chuckled.

"Not bad," he said. "Admire your honesty, Mrs. Addinson. I don't think you'll ever be able to shake Chang, but you might be able to try one angle."

She leaned forward eagerly.

"If there was an association between Chang and your brother, and Chang thinks your brother confided in you, he'll be very edgy," Gideon said. "Edgy men make mistakes. Hm." He hesitated. "Hm, yes." he repeated. "Go along and see him, Mrs. Addinson, give him cause to think you know something. He'll probably try to square you, although he might conceivably try to harm——"

"Oh, he wouldn't dare *that*," she exclaimed. "Not if I told him you were having me followed."

Gideon shook his head sagely.

"You've got a head for this kind of thing," he conceded. "We'll follow you, all right. Go home, Mrs. Addinson, and wait for word from us. We won't keep you long."

They shook hands and he walked with her to the lift. As she went down, he watched and reflected that she was a very fine-looking, finely-built woman.

Five minutes later he'd laid on inquiries about the unknown Estelle, and made arrangements for Foster's sister to be followed. After that he was able to work for twenty minutes without being interrupted.

Perhaps it was going to be a quiet night, after all.

He knew nothing of Alec Fitzroy.

Fitzroy was in his West End flat, not very far from Chang's restaurant, but just outside the fringes of Soho. He stood in the tiny bathroom, shaving. His hand was absolutely steady; he was testing his nerve, making quite sure that it wouldn't let him down.

When he had finished shaving, he felt quite confident.

He left the bathroom, lit a cigarette, and looked at a

decanter of whisky. He wanted a drink, but told himself that it might be a sign of weakness, and that he ought not to have one.

He put the temptation behind him by going into his bedroom. He sat on the side of the bed and went carefully through all the plans to rob the safe deposit in Wattle Street. Nothing was written down, and only he knew all the arrangements for the coup. He did not trust either of his cronies with everything, although they were reliable enough.

It would be necessary to start for the safe deposit building soon. The others, who had further to travel, were already on their way. The escape car was parked—a car which had been left near the Mid-Union Safe Deposit building nightly for several weeks, so there would be nothing unusual about it to-night—except that when it was driven off it would be carrying a fortune.

He checked over every single part of the plan and decided again that it was foolproof.

He jumped up, lit a cigarette, and went into the living-room. This time he didn't argue with himself but poured a tot of whisky and tossed it down. He felt angry because of the word "foolproof"; he told himself that his attitude was completely realistic, and only a fool would call this a job which couldn't go wrong.

It wasn't likely to but it could.

If an inspector or official of the Mid-Union Company were to visit the safe deposit, he would be familiar with all the night staff and, seeing strangers, he would certainly try to raise an alarm. But he'd be bound to ask questions and so give his own identity away. He could be dealt with before doing any harm, like the other members of the night staff would be.

Perhaps it wasn't foolproof; but it certainly wasn't far short.

Fitzroy went back into the bedroom, knelt down in front of a dressing chest, opened the bottom drawer, and rummaged among the underclothes in it.

He drew out a gun and some ammunition. He loaded the

gun, a .32 automatic, and slipped it into his pocket. Then he went and had another whisky. Then he left his flat.

The little widow with whom the Reverend Julian Small lodged watched him as he sat at the table that evening, toying with his food. She was a woman of mercifully few words, one of the few regular churchgoers in the district, and a familiar if faded figure at St. Mary's. She was fond of the new curate, but knew as well as he did that the task was too big for him; at least, he showed no sign that he would ever be able to handle it well.

He was far too gentle.

She was surprised by that in some ways. When his luggage had arrived a few months ago, and she had looked through it, she had found boxing gloves and other things to indicate that he was a dab at games and sports. So when the weedy-looking, rather timid man with the narrow nostrils had arrived on the doorstep, she hadn't realized that it was her lodger.

She had given up hope for him now.

Julian Small had almost given up hope for himself.

He had not properly recovered from the fall that morning. His nose was raw as well as red and painful whenever he touched it, which was often because he had a slight cold. His bitterness had gone, however, and in its place there was a sense of shame—that he should have betrayed his trust as he had; "suffer little children——"

He could not find the way to their confidence or their friendship. It wasn't their fault, it was his.

He did not wholly convince himself of that, but he had one narrow wedge of hope; the Club to-night. It was officially the St. Mary's Club and twenty-odd years old, but when he had arrived there had been the bare hall, a few pieces of damaged furniture, a table tennis top with the plywood warped and chipped, a dart-board so badly eaten away by the darts over the years that some holes showed right through. Small had put all this right. There were three new dart-boards, a regulation-size table-tennis top with trestles, draughts, dominoes, chess, a small library, and, what he regarded as more important than anything else, plenty of comfortable chairs. Thirty youngsters could sit in upholstered comfort and read books or magazines taken from the Club library. There was also a small bar, offering coffee, tea, soft drinks, cakes and biscuits. In fact, everything that a flourishing club of a hundred or so youths could revel in, and——

The Club had *eleven* members.

Usually, most of these failed to appear on Club nights: Mondays, Wednesdays, Fridays and Saturdays. No one had ever said so to the curate, but he believed that the others had been intimidated by youths who didn't come; or else made to feel ridiculous for having anything to do with him.

There was to be a special effort to-night; each member was to try to bring one new member. Until the string incident, Julian Small had told himself that it might be the turn of the tide, and, as he set out from his lodgings for the hall next to the church, he tried to induce a cheerful mood.

Twenty-two lads and lassies instead of one would make all the difference.

Lights were on in the hall.

It was very quiet.

He realized that this was partly due to the fact that the noises of cranes and derricks were missing. So were all the usual sounds which came from the docks by night. He didn't think much about this, but wondered how many would in fact turn up. Twenty-two was absurdly optimistic. Fifteen? Sixteen? He shivered with a kind of excitement as he drew nearer the hall; fifteen would make it a successful evening, and give him hope for the future.

He glanced across at a light fixed to the wall of a ruined warehouse nearby. Some movement by it caught his eye but he couldn't identify the movement. He took no notice until suddenly the warehouse wall light went out.

That made him miss a step.

Tight-lipped, he strode on to the hall. The door was open, light shone out from it, but he saw no one and heard nothing.

He reached it . . .

He stood quite still on the threshold, feeling almost choked. Nothing was in its proper place. The table tennis top was in pieces, strewn about the floor; an axe had been used violently. Pieces of a dart-board were almost under his feet, as small as corks. Books were ripped open, pages strewed the scrubbed floor like pieces of giant confetti. And the chairs——

There wasn't a whole chair left.

He went in, falteringly. He looked round at this savage destruction of his hopes and at the shocking waste of money which he had needed for himself. He looked round, forgetful of his thin, bruised nose, aware only of disaster.

Then, slowly, he spoke to the deserted room.

"If I ever set my hands on them," he said, "I'll break their bloody necks."

Suddenly, without having been given the slightest warning, he felt in a different mood from anything he had known before. He was savagely, viciously angry.

Also, unknown to Gideon, there was Rose Bray.

Rose, at sixteen, was in her first job, and although all of her friends had scoffed when she had said what she was going to do, she was revelling in it. She was a lady's maid. She had a modest but nice little home with her parents in Acton, and had been to school until she was nearly sixteen. She knew shorthand typing and was qualified for many other varieties of jobs, but chose to be a lady's maid.

She liked beautiful clothes.

It was not the kind of liking that creates envy. She was content just to see and handle them, to help dress Lady Muriel, who was nice and natural, not at all like she'd expected real ladies to be—so high falutin' and imperious. "Imperious" was a word which Rose's boy friend had used with great scorn when she had told him what she was going to do.

"These rich people," he had added smartingly, "just a lot of wealthy tarts, that's all they are." And after a moment's pause for research: "Just a lot of *para*sites."

Rose was thinking about her boy friend at the time that

Gideon was looking up at the brown spot in the ceiling, without wondering how it had come there. She was thinking that if Dick only knew Lady Muriel and her husband—who wasn't a Lord or a Sir, she didn't quite understand the reason for that but accepted it—he would have an entirely different idea about the wealthy. Certainly they *were* rich. The diamond necklace which Lady Muriel had left on the dressing-table was worth at least fifteen *years'* wages for her father. The value did not intrigue Rose so much as the beauty, and Rose preferred coloured jewels to diamonds, which seemed to her so cold.

But more than precious stones, she loved the clothes; the rich satins, the smooth velvets, the tulles, the luxurious silks, the colours which were so beautiful that they often made her catch her breath. There were three large wardrobes, all filled with clothes, but Rose's favourites were in the dressing-room: the evening gowns and cocktail dresses.

Sometimes she would open the door, just to look at and to touch the materials.

Many things here had taken some getting used to; this room, for one. It had two doors, one opening into the passage, the other into the bedroom. And across the bedroom, with its two high beds, the rich, soft bedclothes and the twin canopies, each rather like a big baby's crib—was *his* dressing-room. Rose did not go in there much; just occasionally to get something if his valet, Forbes, was out.

Rose did not like Forbes. She could not have explained why, but she didn't trust him.

That evening, Lady Muriel and Mr. Simister were downstairs with friends. About a dozen in all; just a little informal cocktail party, Lady Muriel had said, as she had carelessly selected a dress which had cost over a hundred guineas. Rose was probably one of the few remaining people who could admire such an attitude towards money.

She stood looking at a rich, red velvet gown, and felt irresistibly drawn towards it, longing to smooth the pile of the velvet between her fingers.

She heard a sound in the bedroom.

It did not occur to her that anything was wrong, but she

assumed that Lady Muriel had come upstairs for something she'd forgotten. The carpet on the floor of the dressing-room was thick, muffling the sound of her footsteps as she went towards the communicating door.

She actually began to open it and then saw the man.

He was crouching over the dressing-table. In his right hand was the diamond necklace. There were other jewels in the trinket box which he had taken out of a drawer; a drawer usually kept locked. He didn't look up. She couldn't see his face because of the brown scarf which was drawn up over his nose, but she saw that he wore gloves which looked skin tight.

After the first shock, Rose felt just one thing: fear. It made her want to run away crying for help. Her heart suddenly began to beat so fast that she felt as if she were choking. She knew that her cheeks went chalk-white. She watched, hypnotized, as the man thrust the jewels into a small bag—it looked rather like a chamois-leather, the kind window-cleaners used. She heard the hard stones grate against each other.

She knew what she had to do, if only she could make her legs do what she told them. It was difficult even to turn round. She let the door go, and managed to turn, then stood quite still; her legs simply would not move. Gradually, she made them. She reached the passage door, which was closed, turned the handle and pulled; the door scraped along the carpet and the sound seemed very loud to her.

If only Forbes would come.

She heard no other sound. The big house in Madeson Square overlooking beech and plane trees and a small grass plot where the people of the square aired and exercised their dogs, was solid and silent. A door closed out sound as well as sight.

The passage was carpeted.

She crept out of the dressing-room and now she found that her legs wanted to move too quickly, wanted to run. She dared not. She must go past that door and then downstairs to raise the alarm; if she shouted or if she ran she would warn the thief and he would get away.

Being out here, with the bedroom door closed, she felt safe; excitement replaced the panicky fear. Suddenly she saw herself as the heroine; the girl who had saved Lady Muriel's jewels. It would be easy! She tip-toed towards the door—yes, it was closed, just as it had been when she had passed. It wasn't far to the head of the stairs, and once she reached them she could hurry down.

She drew level with the door.

It opened and the thief grabbed at her.

CHAPTER THIRTEEN

THE THIEF

ROSE saw the door open, the grasping hand, the masked face, in the same awful moment of fear. She opened her mouth wide to scream, but the thief slapped her face. He hurt less than he terrified her. She choked back the scream. He shifted his grip, took her wrist and dragged her into the bedroom.

The door slammed.

"Don't make a sound or I'll break your neck," he growled behind the mask.

She could not have made a sound then, even to save her neck. He was hurting her arm and pulled her across the room towards the beds. *Towards the beds.* Then he changed the direction, first pulled and then pushed her into a corner. She did not realize that here they were safe from the sight of anyone outside, especially the people on the other side of the square.

"Keep your voice low. Have you warned anyone?"

She couldn't get a word out, could only make the shape of the words: "*No, no, no, no, no.*"

"If you're lying to me, I'll——"

"*No, no, no !*"

"You'd better be telling the truth," he said roughly. "Turn round."

"*No !*" That gasp came out.

"Turn round!" he said in a harsh whisper, and pulled at her shoulder. She gasped again and turned helplessly. Then something fell over her head; she started to scream until it reached her mouth, thick and muffling; then it was drawn tight, and she could hardly breathe. Next moment, she felt her hands seized, felt tightness at her wrists, and then realized that he had tied her wrists together behind her.

He spun her round again.

"Sit down," he said, and before she could realize what the order meant, he bent down and picked her up, then dumped her heavily on the floor. With her hands behind her she couldn't get up easily. The scarf or whatever it was still forced itself into her mouth, and she was struggling for breath.

He left her.

He must have spent another three or four minutes at the dressing-table, cramming things into the wash-leather bag. Then he turned away, and took notice of her again. She had not recovered from the first fear and all this made it much, much worse.

"Now what am I going to do with you?" he said softly. "If you raise the alarm——"

He came towards her slowly. She wanted to cry out that she wouldn't raise the alarm, if only he would go she'd never say a word to anyone; but she couldn't utter a sound of any kind. He stood looking down at her. He wasn't really very big, but from that angle he looked enormous, and she was absolutely in his power. All the stories of murder she had ever heard about seemed to flash through her mind.

"Get up," he said, as if he had made up his mind what to do, and she cringed away from him. He bent down, took her waist, and pulled her to her feet. Then he pushed her towards the dressing-room. Her legs moved automatically, she thought she was bound to fall on her face.

The lovely clothes were in the wardrobe.

"Just the job," he said, and hustled her forward. "Get in." He meant, "get into the wardrobe with the clothes." "Go on, Rosie, get in, I won't hurt you!"

She was breathing through her nose, and felt as if she could never breathe freely again, was almost choked. And she was too frightened to believe what he said. Something made him change his mind, too. He stretched out an arm to her shoulder, turned her round, and loosened the scarf round her mouth; it dropped to her neck.

"My, my," he said, "you're quite something, pity we didn't meet some other place."

Suddenly he pulled her to him and squeezed her. She felt

his hard, lean body, the thudding of his heart. She felt the surge of desire in him, too, and a different fear began to choke her. She couldn't breathe, she felt his hands——

He let her go.

"Get inside," he said harshly, "and if you open your trap for the next five minutes, you'll wish you'd never been born."

He thrust her back among the luxurious dresses, among thousands of pounds' worth of the most exclusive models by the world's great designers, and then closed the door. She heard the key in the lock. She leaned back against a velvet gown, slipping further and further down, still frightened, and also disturbed in a different way. She could not forget the hardness of his body against her.

Then she slipped down until she was almost full length on the floor. With her hands behind her, she could turn round. It was blackly dark. She felt herself breathing evenly, but fear soon began to catch up, like the sea sweeping over her in waves.

She shouted and the sound was muffled, she knew that it couldn't be heard.

She started to struggle and to shout, and was terrified. The blackness became thick, oily, choking, throttling; the blackness became peopled with strange shapes, strange, bright, dazzling, blinding colours. After a while she was screaming without knowing what she was doing . . .

Then the door opened:

"Good Lord!" exclaimed Lady Muriel's husband. "What —here, Inspector, here's the maid, here she is!"

Rose felt much better.

Everyone had been very kind, especially Lady Muriel and Mr. Simister. The police had been quite nice, too. The man Mr. Simister called Inspector was ever so young, really. She'd had some hot coffee, very sweet, and then a weak whisky and water, and the doctor—Lady Muriel's own doctor—had been and examined her, and said that she wouldn't suffer much harm. Then the Inspector had started to question her, making her remember everything she had seen and everything that had been said. She didn't like it.

Twice Lady Muriel asked him if it were really necessary, and in a firm but friendly way he said it was essential.

Then something he said made her remember that the thief had called her Rosie.

"Are you sure?" The Inspector's voice sharpened.

"Oh, yes! Of course I am."

"How often did he use your name?"

"Well, only once, I remember . . ."

A few minutes afterwards, the Inspector spoke to Mr. Simister in a voice which Rose was supposed not to hear but which she heard quite clearly:

"If it's someone who knew the name of the maid, it suggests co-operation from your staff. And a key to the trinket box was used, remember. I think I'd better see the staff at once, Mr. Simister, especially anyone who knew this suite well."

Lady Muriel said in a startled voice: "Not *Forbes*."

"Don't be silly, darling," Mr. Simister said sharply.

There was a moment almost of conflict; then Lady Muriel turned to Rose.

"You look tired, Rose, and I'm sure the Inspector won't want you any more now." Her glance at the Inspector suggested that he had better not. "Come along to the morning room, and I'll get you something."

She put a hand on Rose's arm.

It was rather wonderful, Rose thought, walking side by side with Lady Muriel, who was a head taller, very, *very* beautiful, and wearing that lovely cocktail gown which was full of rich colours. It was almost like walking alongside a friend.

Behind them, Mr. Simister was talking worriedly to the Inspector.

The office was stuffy. April was behaving oddly, you could usually rely on a chilly evening, but even with the windows open it was warm. Gideon had his coat off, his waistcoat open, his tie hanging down, his sleeves rolled up. For once his hair was ruffled. He was talking first into one telephone and then into another, putting down and lifting receivers as if he were juggling with Indian clubs. The smooth transi-

tion from one case to the next came much in the way that a
brilliant linguist can change from one language to another
without any apparent interruption in thought.

And Gideon made notes.

"That you, Adams—anything doing in the Madeson
Square job? . . . Hmm . . . No, don't bring the valet over here
unless you're pretty sure he's involved, no need to put a foot
wrong. . . . Yes, old chap, watch him if you like. . . . How's
that maid, what's her name? . . . Yes, Rose . . . Good. Any
prints? . . . Hmm, looks as if the valet's the chief hope.
'Bye."

There was hardly a pause before he turned to the other
telephone, already in his left hand.

"Hallo, Lem, sorry to keep you. Any luck? . . ." He
chuckled. "And you stood Fifi up for this, you're going to
know all about it! . . . I know it's not funny, calm down . . .
Well, stay there if you like, we certainly want that chap.
Think he's been along already and noticed that the car's
being watched? . . . Who've you got with you?"

The other bell started to ring. Gideon lifted the receiver
and switched to it swiftly: "Hold on, please." He went back
to Lemaitre. "Well, he doesn't look so much like a copper as
some of 'em. Give it another hour. 'Bye."

"Hallo . . .?

"Oh, Fred, thanks for calling. Any news of Birdy? . . .
Pity . . . Found that junk at his house, did you? Well,
spread the story round, won't you, then if we pick him up his
friends and neighbours will know it's because he's wanted; it
won't look as if he came to us for protection. . . . No, I know
he didn't. . . . So do I."

There was a moment's lull.

"So do I," he repeated, and meant that he hoped that the
Divisional people found Birdy.

The hell of this was that a gang like Murphy's could act
almost with impunity; *almost*.

He pulled his wad of notes towards him. These were the
scribbled notes he had started to make from the moment
he'd come in that morning. Everything that had been at-
tended to he crossed off; only half a dozen items remained,

and he wrote these out on a fresh slip of paper. They were mostly trifles, and among them was:

Check Basil B. about his evidence on the Moxley job.

He lifted a receiver.

"Know if Chief Inspector Boardman's in?" he said. "Oh —ring his home for me, will you?" He put the receiver down and waited; the other bell rang. "Hallo, Gideon here. Eh? . . . Good Lord!" He found himself chuckling, looked as if he were delighted. "Nice work, glad they don't always get away with it." He chuckled again, and then saw the office door open. "Yes, I'll put some dynamite behind them, but King-Hadden's off duty to-night, it's never so quick when——"

The visitor was the Assistant Commissioner, his sleek grey suit changed to sleek dinner jacket, soft cream shirt, small bow tie; a distinguished man indeed.

". . . okay, Basil," Gideon said, and rang off and looked up smiling. "Didn't expect you back," he remarked.

"I had a dinner date I couldn't miss," the A.C. said, "but wanted an excuse to cut the speeches. How are things going?"

"It's like rain," said Gideon, and then corrected himself. "Hailstorm, rather."

"With an occasional rainbow—what's so funny?"

Gideon chuckled.

"Chap broke into a house in Maida Vale an hour ago, a six-footer apparently, and he had a gun. The woman of the house discovered him and chased him out with an umbrella. He dropped the gun! Empty. Evans was telling me, he can always make a story like that sound twice as funny as it is, but——" Gideon chuckled. "Armed gunman chased by angry woman with umbrella—can't you see the headlines in the morning? It'll keep something off the front page."

"The Waterloo job, I hope."

"Not much chance of that." Gideon grimaced and told what had happened.

"You've always thought that there was organization in these mail van jobs, haven't you?" the A.C. asked musingly.

"Some sort of," agreed Gideon. "The pattern's always

pretty well the same, isn't it? I'd say that there's a clearing house for information, which always reaches the same chap. He passes it on to different people, and they give him a rake-off. First time I've ever been hopeful is to-day, if Chang——"

He broke off.

The A.C. lit a cigarette.

"I was wondering," he said, sitting on the arm of the easy chair reserved for visitors. "You've thought that it was worth giving Chang rope, haven't you? Any special reason?"

"You mean, when I heard about Foster from Birdy, why didn't I go for Chang straightaway?" Gideon pinched his nose. "I don't know. Don't suppose I ever shall. I just felt it was the wrong thing to do, but I'm not so sure now. But see what's working out. Birdy squealed on Chang. Chang has put a finger on him, through Murphy. That gives a direct line between Chang and Murphy. Now we know that Murphy is nominal boss of a gang, and that among the people who do jobs for him there's every kind of crook, from killer to snatch artist. Well, if Chang is the man who gets the information about mail vans and passes it on to Murphy, Murphy might pass it further down. I don't say it is the answer, just that it could be. The one certain thing about Murphy's bunch is that they're tough and they're smart and they don't squeal. We've been trying to get Murphy for years, have never pulled him in on anything that counted, and haven't thought it worth while putting him inside for a couple of months. Now, we've got a half chance of picking up one of the men who did the Waterloo job to-day, and if we can lead back from him to Murphy we might really have something."

Gideon paused.

"Yes, you would," agreed the A.C. fervently.

"If we could get Murphy and hit him really hard it would do more good than we've done at one swipe for months," said Gideon, as if he longed for exactly that. "For *years*. Meanwhile, we've started a new line. I've sent out instructions for all known Murphy men to be checked and to find out if any of them have postmen among their friends. I'm

having Chang's customers checked, too, to find out if there
are any postmen among them. Or bank managers or clerks,
for that matter. It's the first time we've thought of Chang or
Murphy together or singly as in any way interested in the
mail van jobs. Could be wrong now, but at least it's giving us
a bit of pep for the time being."

"George," said the A.C., "I have never suggested that you
don't know your job."

Gideon grinned.

"Thanks! Then there's another angle. Foster's sister
had a telephone call from a hysterical woman who said that
Foster had been murdered." He deliberately ignored the
A.C.'s start of surprise. "Woman named Estelle, apparently
a sweetie of Foster's. I started to check, and one of the girls
who dance at Chang's club is named Estelle."

"Well, well," murmured the A.C. "Talked to her yet?"

"Haven't found her. She digs in Chelsea, but hasn't been
home since morning. As soon as we get a chance, we'll tackle
her."

A telephone bell rang, almost before he had finished.

"Excuse me," he said, and plucked the receiver up.
"Gideon . . . *What?*" He bellowed the word, must have
deafened the man at the other end of the line, and certainly
startled the A.C. "Bring him right over," he said, only a
little less boomingly, "nice work, Lem! Wonderful!"

He put the receiver down. The Assistant Commissioner,
who knew him in most moods, had seldom seen him show
such obvious satisfaction; and that could only come from
really good news.

Gideon appeared to want to savour it before passing it on.

"We've got the driver of the Austin with the Michelin
tyre," he said at last, and his expression said: 'How about
that?" "Young chap with a scar at the back of his head—
the Waterloo post office driver saw a chap like that, remember." Gideon was more excited than the A.C. had seen him
for years, but he fought against showing it. "Lemaitre's
bringing him over. Going to sit in in this interview, sir?" He
grinned almost impudently.

The A.C. said: "I think I will, George. That's fine."

"But it's late to have that post-office driver in," decided Gideon, and his pencil sped. "We'll have an identification parade at ten o'clock in the morning. I wonder if this could be *the* day." He got up to stretch his cramped limbs. "I think a noggin's indicated here. Going to have one?"

"On principle and in office hours," said the A.C., "I disapprove. But thanks." The telephone rang. "All right, I'll get the whisky," he said, and rounded the desk as Gideon picked up the receiver.

"Gideon here."

"Oh . . . "

"Yes, all right. 'Bye." Gideon rang off and kept a finger on the cradle of the telephone as the A.C. stooped to open a cupboard in one of the pedestals of his desk. "Fire out at Mince Lane, a big fur warehouse. The fire chief thinks it might be arson. I'd better send Marjoribanks over." He lifted a receiver. "Detective-Inspector Marjoribanks, please. . . . Hallo, Marj, got nice job for you, Belinda Blue-eyes thinks that there's arson in Mince Lane—pretty well gutted a warehouse, I gather, have a go as soon as you can."

"Thanks," he added a minute later, and then put the receiver down and took a glass from the A.C., who held a syphon in his right hand. "Splash more, I think," he said, and watched the soda water as it squirted and splashed. "Whoa! Ta. Here's to getting a trail back from this to Chang or Murphy." He ran his tongue along his lips. "No more news of Birdy, I'm worried about that. I—oh, *damn the blurry telephone!*"

"If I were you," said the A.C., "I'd get out for a bit and leave a sergeant in here."

"Blurry sergeants! . . . Gideon . . . Eh? . . . Oh, not bad, but he can keep until morning, hold him at Cannon Row, will you? It won't do him any harm to wriggle a bit. Yes, I'll hold on. It's Percival, from London Airport," he told the A.C. offhandedly. "That Foreign Office chap who pinched the diplomatic bag from the *sanctum sanctorum's* turned up, complete with bag. It's still full, so we do get results sometimes." He scribbled. "Must let the Press have that quickly, especially the *Globe*, it's been screaming about missing diplomats for two years. Or is it three?" Into the telephone he said, "Violent, is he? Well, get some help, don't let him cut his throat. 'Bye."

He rang off.

"You rather remind me," said the A.C., supping his whisky and soda, "of a bulldozer which never stops moving."

"Don't say that in anyone's hearing or I'll be the Bulldozer for the rest of my stay here, which I sometimes hope won't be long!"

Gideon grinned.

He rang the Back Room Inspector to tell them about the arrest of the diplomat.

He had time to light his pipe.

He picked up a telephone at the first ting of the bell.

"Gideon . . . Oh, yes . . . Oh, lor'. I hate those jobs. Can you handle it yourself? . . . Yes, you'll have to stop him, I suppose, fix it with the stations, ports and airports, but soft pedal a bit." He rang off, forgetting to say " 'bye". "That was about Eric Rosenthal—he and his wife have been having a tug-o'-war with their kid, remember. The wife got a court order for custody, and Rosenthal snatched her this evening. What will a thing like this do to a six-year-old girl?"

He shook his head.

He thought of Kate.

The telephone rang.

This time it was news with a vengeance. The man Fessell, wanted in connection with the murder of the old woman in the Islington sweet shop, had been seen in Watford. He should be caught before long.

Then Gideon thought of Birdy Merrick.

He didn't think of a man named Fitzroy, for he had never heard of him.

CHAPTER FOURTEEN

THE MURPHY GANG DRAWS CLOSE

BIRDY stood in a dark doorway. Gaslight showed white and pure behind the glass of a lamp fastened to a wall by an iron bracket. Nearby, the ripple of the water of a backwater of the Thames sounded softly and insistently, as if someone were whispering to him. A long way off there was another whisper of sound: traffic on the Mile End and the White-chapel Roads.

The river traffic was silent.

It was not often silent, like this; usually a tug chugged along or hooted; or cargo ships laden down to the Plimsoll line sent their short, urgent blasts to tell the Port of London Authority officials that they were on their way to distant lands. Or a police launch barked on its urgent, questing note, and a searchlight swept the dark, dirty water, looking for unexpected things; or else expected jetsam, such as floating bodies.

This silence was accursed. In it every little sound could be heard, and Birdy knew that two of Murphy's men were near him—listening. Their ears were as sensitive to the night sounds of London as a bushman's would be for the night sounds of the forest.

No cranes were working.

The silence was so deep that Birdy could have screamed; and screaming brought on death or whatever they planned for him.

Why weren't the cranes busy?

Birdy remembered: there was a strike. Not a full-blooded one, but a nasty, mean little strike—no overtime. Birdy had heard dockers talking about it, some for and some against; but they all obeyed. There was no trade union in crime, criminals were self-employed, uninsured and independent. Now, that awful hush fell upon dockland and upon Birdy.

He had wormed his way here after seeing Lefty, and waited for the blessed fall of darkness. He had felt that he dared hope, and stood in the doorway, listening for protecting noises which would not come—and listening, too, for the stealthy sounds which might tell of Ali or the Snide.

The Snide was a knife artist, too.

Lefty was a broken bottle artist.

Down at the foot of the steps at Aldgate Station there had been—a razor artist. So Birdy had a good idea what to expect. They were going to cut him up. Chang had given the word because he had squealed, and now Murphy's gang were going to cut him up.

It would be better to kill himself.

He heard a soft, swift footfall.

His hands went up to his breast, clenched fearfully; his ears strained the quiet, his eyes tried to probe the darkness beyond the clear glow of the gas-lamp.

It came again—stealthy, nearer.

A voice whispered: *"Come on, Birdy, we've got you cornered."*

That was the Snide. The Snide had once been an artist in making lead coins, sludge, snide, call it what you liked; but now he preferred that knife. He wasn't so good as Ali, but he was good.

The sneering, mocking whisper came again.

"We've got you cornered."

Everything Birdy knew, everything he sensed, worked in him for his own protection now. Thirty years of East End slum life, most of it with one of the gangs or another—not a fighting member, just a hanger-on—had told him plenty. He knew London and Londoners and Ali and the Snide. That whisper was to work on his nerves, to lure him out of his doorway, to make him run *away* from the sound; and if he did that he would run into Ali. There might be others, too; he had been crouching here for ten minutes, plenty of time for reinforcements to creep up.

"Give it up, Birdy."

"What part of you shall we send home to Ethel, Birdy?"

The Snide always tormented like this; he'd had an education and liked to demonstrate it.

"*Come on, Birdy——*"

Birdy fingered a sardine tin in his coat pocket; he'd picked
it up from the kerb at dusk, and it was a weapon of sorts; not
of attack but of defence by ruse. He nicked his finger on the
torn edge. He didn't wince but flinched.

The Snide was very near.

Ali . . .?

In a moment or two they would rush him.

Birdy raised the sardine tin, moving it round in his fingers
until he found a smooth section which he could grip. He
made a few silent swinging motions with his arm and then
tossed the can into the air. It made a funny little twittering
noise, the others must wonder what it was. Then there was a
hush; then the tin clanged upon the road on the other side
of the street.

Birdy darted out of his cover.

In that split second the Snide would be distracted; at least
he ought to be. He would look towards the sound and Ali
would probably do the same thing. That would be Birdy's
chance, his only one. He darted out of the doorway and was
revealed for a moment in the white glow.

He saw the Snide, a thin face turned towards the sardine
tin. He did not see Ali, but guessed that Ali was behind him.

He leapt forward.

The Snide swung round, the knife glittered. Birdy was
very close. He felt the knife cut through his shoulder and
then he drove his knee into the pit of the Snide's stomach
with sickening force and with the accuracy of an expert. He
heard the Snide give a groan that was torturing in its
anguish, in its tale of sickening pain. The Snide slid away
from him, and Birdy raced on towards the corner, the docks,
the ships where he hoped to find refuge.

He heard Ali.

He looked over his shoulder and saw the dark shape of the
lascar, and his long shadow cast by the gaslight.

Then he saw a man in front of him.

Lefty? . . .

Birdy's heart seemed to stop.

Lefty.

He swerved to one side. Lefty moved towards him with the extra speed of twenty-one to forty-one. Birdy was sure, then, that he hadn't a chance. He ran on blindly. He felt Lefty's outstretched hand pluck at his sleeve, but tore himself free. Now all he could do was to run until he fell in his tracks. There was no hope, but he had to go on until they fell upon him and carved him up—or tore him to pieces. Hounds after a fox. Hounds——

He became aware of a different, moving light, coming towards him, bright beams sweeping the street. A blue light showed at the top of the car, with the word *Police*. Birdy could just make out the shapes of the two men in the car.

He heard nothing behind him, but he knew that Lefty and Ali had turned away in fright. They might help the Snide or they might leave the Snide to be picked up.

Birdy waited until the car had passed him and then began to hurry towards the docks. He could get into a crane, or sneak aboard one of the ships; he might even swim across to the other side of the Thames. He'd done it before.

That was unless a Murphy man was watching him now; or waiting for him in the shadows ahead.

Gideon, his tie knotted loosely, coat on, shirt cuffs undone, bloodshot eyes obviously very tired, and hat on the back of his head, looked at the sergeant who had just come in. He had nothing against the sergeant; nothing against sergeants as a general rule. But you got the fool sometimes, and he had had two or three bright specimens that day: this seemed to be his moment of misfortune.

"Yes, put every message on paper," he said, "and make sure that anything that different sections ought to have, reaches them quickly."

The tow-haired sergeant, who was old enough to know better, said timidly:

"What kind of things, sir?"

Gideon managed not to swear, tried to phrase what he meant simply, and was almost relieved that the telephone bell rang. He turned back to the desk to pick up the receiver, knowing that he ought to leave this call to the sergeant. Lemaitre and the others were downstairs with the prisoner with the scarred head; a man named Mazzioni. In a fury of checking, the Yard knew that Mazzioni had no record in London, and copies of his prints were being made to send to the Provinces. The A.C. was downstairs, waiting for Gideon, and a blockhead of a sergeant——

"Gideon . . . Oh, hallo, Fred." This was the one call he was glad he'd taken, after all; and he was surprised that he felt really on edge. "Anything?"

"Yes and no," said the G5 Superintendent. "One of my patrols picked up the Snide. He had a couple of knives in his pocket, with traces of blood on one——"

Gideon winced.

"—— but Birdy got away," the Superintendent went on. "Our chaps saw him as he headed for the docks. He's as slippery as they come, and as frightened as hell."

"I'd be frightened, in his shoes," said Gideon heavily.

"Who wouldn't?"

"Well, thanks, Fred," Gideon said. "We picked up a chap in connection with the Waterloo job, by the way, and may have some luck."

"Here's to it," the other man said.

Gideon put the receiver down, and looked up at the sergeant, forgetting to glare; the man was at Lemaitre's desk, with a telephone in his hand.

Gideon found himself chuckling.

He nodded and went out. Half-way along the passage he remembered that the sergeant seemed to be confident enough now, scribbling something in so fast that it must have been in shorthand. A job in hand was a fine nerve tonic.

Now for Mazzioni.

Mazzioni looked tough.

You could pick them out, and it was obvious from Lemaitre's manner that he had picked Mazzioni out, quickly enough. For the man was handcuffed with his hands in front of him. He was hatless, and swarthy—no, olive-skinned; not one of the good-looking Italians. He was either Italian or of Italian extraction, Gideon knew, and when Italians came bad they were often very, very bad.

Mazzioni was shorter than medium height, and not particularly broad; really, a small man but very upright. It was obvious that he was physically fit; his poise somehow made that clear. He had a broad, flattened nose, obviously broken many years before, fine eyes, thick, jet black hair and jet black eyebrows. He needed a shave. His lips were parted and showed a glimpse of white teeth; he had that caged, criminal-at-bay look which the really vicious criminals had, and Gideon thought he had something else: the look of a dopey.

There was a nasty graze, bleeding a little, on his right temple.

Lemaitre said: "He made a fight of it, that's where he got marked. Plenty of witnesses."

Lemaitre no longer sounded cock-a-hoop; it was as if he knew that Mazzioni wasn't going to be a lot of help. There was the kind who would talk under pressure and the kind who wouldn't, and it was usually easy to pick these out, too. In Lemaitre's words as well as his manner there was a hint of frustration, and a thing which everyone at the Yard or on the Force anywhere suffered from: fear that they would be accused of exceeding their duty. A prisoner with a bruised face was a prisoner with an angry, vengeful counsel. Once convince a jury that a man had been ill-treated, and the odds against a conviction——

Gideon checked himself.

The A.C. wasn't here after all.

"When's the Old Man coming?" he asked.

"Just rang, won't be a minute," Lemaitre answered.

Gideon nodded.

Mazzioni looked from him to Lemaitre and back again. He wasn't sure what to make of this or what they would make of him. He would be happier if either of them talked; this silence, this cold appraisal from the newcomer, was an unsettling, disturbing thing. And Gideon, looking like a great bear and glowering as if the bear were angry, didn't mind how much he worked on the prisoner's nerves.

Was he a dopey?

There was a tap at the door. A uniformed constable looked in.

"All okay, sir."

"Thanks," said Gideon.

That meant that the A.C. was in position, able to listen to what was being said, and looking into the room through a window which appeared to be opaque from the inside. They were ready to start.

But as he looked at Mazzioni, with his first question on his lips, Gideon felt suddenly hopeless, although it was hard to say why. It was partly because he was tired; not flogged out, as he was sometimes, but flagging badly; the day had caught up with him. It was partly because of the ugly look in Mazzioni's eyes, too, the certainty that this was a tough nut.

This interrogation was going to last a long time.

Lemaitre had his notebook out. Lemaitre, after his burst of triumph, felt much the same as Gideon; catching your man was only the beginning, and in this case it didn't look like the promising beginning they had hoped.

Lemaitre had been going to take his Fifi out.

He'd be lucky if he were home by midnight. So would Gideon.

The hell of it was that this was just another day.

Mazzioni didn't talk, but two things made Gideon very thoughtful. A police-surgeon said that he was certainly addicted to cocaine, and at Mazzioni's rooms in Bethnal Green the Divisional police found a packet of reefers and a small packet of cocaine.

CHAPTER FIFTEEN

WORRIED MEN

CHANG was worried.

He was in his office, with ledgers open in front of him, for his best love was to work over the figures of his businesses. Then the news of Mazzioni's capture reached him by telephone. It was a whispered statement, briefly made, as if the speaker were eager to get the message delivered and be off. He put the receiver down stealthily, and there was silence on the line and in Chang's office.

Chang now wore a dinner jacket, beautifully cut, a white shirt and a purple bow-tie. His sparse black hair glistened with brilliantine. The light in the ceiling cast soft shadows of his prominent eyebrows and his nose over his face, giving him an oddly sinister look. His lips were parted but not visible to anyone who happened to look at him. He sat quite still, a faintly yellow hand resting on the open pages of the ledger, in which he was keeping records of restaurant trade: or so the ledger's legend said. For tea, Chang read reefers; for deliveries of tea he read marihuana or hashish, whichever was available. Occasionally it was dagga from Africa, and the effect of this was much the same, with dagga perhaps more harsh than the others.

"Coffee" and cocaine were synonymous.

All this afforded Chang deep amusement most of the time, for he could safely allow the police to study these records. Until that morning, at all events, he had felt sure that there was no risk. With Foster at Scotland Yard, biddable under the twin pressures of greed and fear, with several key men in banks and post offices throughout London, and with his own carefully conceived plan to block every line of inquiry which might lead to him, he had felt that nothing could go wrong.

He was less sure now. Foster's telephone call, his sister's

prying visit, Gideon's call and then a hysterical outburst from the dancer, Estelle, had combined to give him a very bad day. It was Estelle who had betrayed the fact that Birdy had found out and squealed. Now, Birdy was on the run, and so was the dancer.

Murphy was after them both.

Chang did not think Birdy could be dangerous, and knew that it had been a mistake to set Murphy on to the squealer. The police knew about it by now; and Murphy's contact men were unable to concentrate on the search for Estelle, whose knowledge could be deadly; could, in fact, hang him.

Chang had not realized that Estelle was in love with Foster.

Chang sat quite motionless in the small, warm office. No sound came from the café, although a radiogram was playing soft, rhythmic music in there, and occasionally a crooner sang. No reefers were being sold, the soft drinks were not pepped up, yet any Yard man who came in, any doctor who knew the signs, and any victim of the dream-drugs, would know that half of the people here were dopies. From their bright eyes, they would have known that they had recently had a drag or a shot.

Chang did not think of these things.

Chang, in his way, was very like Gideon. He had the same kind of mind, the same tight grasp of situations and circumstances, the same unfailing memory and the same intentness. For Gideon, there was the reward of doing his job, for Chang the reward of making a fortune; but to each the actual task was the very pulse of life. In Gideon the chief thing was the task of seeking the criminal and hunting him down, of making sure that he could never strike again to hurt, to rob, to frighten or to maim. In Chang, the attraction was the plotting against the police, the moves in a game as in a game of chess or Mah Jong—wits against wits, and the amassing of a fortune.

The police had become his natural enemy.

They had suspected him for a long time, but with Foster in his pocket he had known that he was temporarily secure. Others were also in his pocket. He was ringed round with

men, a few of whom knew that they served him, most of
whom did not know that their instructions came from him.
"Instructions" was too often the wrong word. Hints, tip-
offs, suggestions, help in emergency—all of these came
through Chang, and for reward he received a share of whatever profit was made. His share was passed on to him. Sometimes it was handed over, in cash, at the café; or to other,
smaller cafés where he had contacts in the East and West
Ends, in Chelsea, in Bloomsbury.

There was Chang with supplies for his cafés, all legitimate
business on the surface. Here was Chang, deeply worried.
Estelle was anxiety enough, but he had trained himself to
concentrate on one thing at a time, and the greatest anxiety
was the captured Italian.

Chang knew Mazzioni personally and Mazzioni knew him;
so he could betray him to the police. The Italian's record
was good, because Chang had saved him from a charge
several times, but reputation went for nothing once the police
were working on you. Mazzioni might crack and talk to save
himself.

Never trust anyone, Chang believed, unless you could
compel them to serve faithfully.

Mazzioni was out of his reach.

Mazzioni's wife wasn't.

How should he deal with the Italian? Could he find a way
of warning him of the consequences of failure?

No, Chang decided, not that; not yet. Mazzioni was
tough and he would hold out for some time, he might hold
out for a long time. He took an occasional sniff of snow, but
could get along without it. The way to make sure of
Mazzioni's loyalty was to promise him help. Help, for instance, for his pretty young wife; then help with the
police.

Chang did not know how the Italian had been picked up.
He knew that he had done the job at Waterloo, and that
most of the money had already been safely salted away; but
Mazzioni might have been caught with some of the money on
him. The police might find indisputable evidence of his
complicity, but they might be taking a chance. If Mazzioni

had an alibi, it could make all the difference to the way the case went.

Chang lifted the telephone, dialled a number, and waited. He had to wait for a long time. *Brrr-brrr, brrr-brrr.* It was too long. Possessed of all the calm of his unknown ancestors, he began to bare his teeth; but then the call was answered, a man said breathlessly:

"Mayfair 29451."

"Mr. Ledbetter," Chang said softly, "it is urgent that I should see you."

"Who——"

"An old friend, Mr. Ledbetter."

There was a moment's silence; then the man spoke again, in a voice less breathless but quite empty of pleasure.

"Oh, I know. Look, can't it wait? I have some friends here. In the morning——"

"I am sorry, Mr. Ledbetter, it is urgent. Meet me in Room 217 at the Occident Hotel, please."

"But I can't——"

"It is very urgent, Mr. Ledbetter," Chang said.

Ledbetter answered gruffly: "Oh, all right."

Chang rang off without another word. He lifted the receiver again, almost at once. His movement was quick yet graceful, very different from Gideon's grab; and his hand was half the size of Gideon's.

A woman answered.

"Mary," Chang greeted, "this afternoon, between two o'clock and four o'clock, where were you?"

"Hallo, Chin," said the woman, in a deep, throaty voice. "I was at Kingston. Didn't anyone tell you, I'm at Kingston every afternoon? It's one of the places where I work." There was laziness and laughter in her voice, one would picture a big, hearty, fleshy woman, sensuous, good-hearted, quick-witted.

"Understand," said Chang, "you were at Kingston and a good friend of yours was there, also, with you. Mazzioni."

"Maz? Why, he——"

"He was with you, please remember, all the time."

The woman laughed.

"His little sweetie pie won't like that!"

"His little sweetie pie," mimicked Chang, "will not worry about it this time. Now, please understand. He arrived at two, he left at four, there is no mistake. Find one, find even two people to say that also."

"Okay, Chin," the woman said. "Bad trouble?"

"It could be."

"What I do for my men," said the woman named Mary.

Chang rang off. He sat quite still again, until his left hand moved to the inside pocket of his beautifully cut coat. He took out a tiny lacquered snuff box, with a beautiful garden design, pressed, opened it, and took a tiny pinch of white snuff. He put this on to the back of his hand and sniffed it up each nostril; then he replaced the box slowly. He stood up, stretched for his hat, and went out of the office.

A girl was in the little cloakroom on the landing, and the radiogram was playing swing. Shuffling footsteps told of people dancing. The ordinary, clean smell of tobacco smoke wafted towards him.

"Has Estelle telephoned?"

"No, sir."

"I will be back soon," Chang said.

"Okay."

He went downstairs, passing a coloured photograph of Estelle. She had long, rippling red hair and a big, white smile and quite beautiful legs. Chang only glanced in passing. Nodding to a flat-faced waiter, he turned into the spotless kitchen, where the Chinese staff looked at him without expression, and he behaved as if no one was there. He went out of the little back door and slipped swiftly along a passage towards Middle Street.

At Middle Street he had a shock.

A plainclothes man was on the other side of the road; and there was only one reason why he should be there.

Chang felt even more worried.

He smiled across at the man, and turned into Middle Street, then made his way towards Shaftesbury Avenue. He was followed, and was worried chiefly because the police

were so interested. He would have to be very, very careful.

Had it been a mistake to run Foster down?

If so, it had been Mazzioni's mistake, too; that was the
chief source of worry. Mazzioni had been at hand when
Foster had telephoned. Foster had been scared, and had
talked of squealing unless Chang promised help. In a quick
flood of annoyance and alarm, Chang had made his mistake
by telling Mazzioni what to do, and Mazzioni had acted too
quickly, and too close to Soho.

Chang thought belatedly of other things that had turned
out to be mistakes, too; letting Estelle know that Foster was
in his pay, for instance; and forgetting that she had been
here for a rehearsal, when he had given Mazzioni his orders.

At Piccadilly Circus, Chang slipped the sergeant who was
on his tail, but knew that there might be others on the look-
out for him. He was conspicuous, like any Chinese. Piccadilly Circus always had its policemen, its plainclothes men,
its police spies, and if they had been told to watch for Chang
it would be dangerous.

Chang got into a taxi. He did not think that he was followed as he was taken to the restaurant entrance of the
Occident Hotel. There was not likely to be a detective lurk-
ing at this side, but there was sure to be a hotel dick if not a
policeman in the foyer.

He went through a service door to service stairs and then
up to Room 217. This was reserved in the name of Smith,
and a Mr. Smith had come, signed the register, and left the
hotel, sending the key to Chang. It would be a rendezvous
for a week; then there would be another hotel, another room.

When Ledbetter came, he also looked worried. He was a
big, lusty man with iron grey hair, quite distinguished in his
way. He had a very good reputation, was an astute lawyer,
and had made one mistake; a little matter of embezzlement.
No one yet knew, except Chang and a clerk in Ledbetter's
office who was aware that Chang liked that kind of information.

Chang looked very small beside him.

"Well, what is it?" Ledbetter didn't like Chinese, didn't

like anyone whose skin was yellow or brown or black. He was as massive as Gideon, well-dressed, scowling, resentful. The furrows in his forehead added to the touch of distinction.

"There is a very urgent matter," Chang said. He found it easy to smile, especially at men whom one disliked. "A friend of mine, named Marco Mazzioni, has been arrested by the police. He is a very good friend, and it would be dangerous for many people if he were to be tried. It is believed that he was connected with the mail van robbery this afternoon, but that is ridiculous—he was at Kingston, with Mary Clayton. You know Mary."

Ledbetter said: "Did he do the job?"

"You have to see him," said Chang, still smiling. "Just see him, and tell him that he need not worry. Mary will tell the truth and say that he was with her from two o'clock until four. You understand?"

Ledbetter said: "I don't like it, Chang. If the police can prove that he wasn't——"

"Then, Mary lied to you," said Chang. "Do not be foolish, Mr. Ledbetter. This is an urgent matter. See your friends at Scotland Yard at once, please."

He smiled . . .

Ledbetter went out, obviously as worried as when he came in, much more resentful, but undoubtedly prepared to be obedient. Chang went to a telephone by the side of the bed. He looked very short. He hesitated for a moment, partly because he was thinking of Ledbetter. He knew that the solicitor regarded him as a yellow-skinned savage; he also knew that Ledbetter was in a very tight fix.

Chang telephoned Mazzioni's wife.

A man with a deep voice answered, almost certainly a policeman; in fact, Chang felt quite sure. He spoke promptly and in a deep voice from which he kept all trace of accent.

"Mrs. Mazzioni, please."

"Who wants her?"

"A friend."

There was a moment's pause; then the mutter of men's voices; then Mazzioni's wife came on the line. Chang knew her for a pretty, fluffy-haired blonde, with a jealous temperament.

She sounded scared.

"Who's that?"

"Of course, you know of the accident to your husband," Chang said, still sounding "English". "But it will be all right, my dear. You will find out that he was with Mary at Kingston all the afternoon. There is no need to worry at all. That is the perfect alibi, you see."

"The perfect——"

"That is the police with you, I believe," Chang said. "They will ask who called. Say I am a friend, to tell you of what happened to Maz. And one other thing, little one— when the police ask if you know where Maz was this afternoon, be angry. Do you understand?" He paused, but only for a moment. "Be *very* angry, say he was going to see that bitch Mary at Kingston." Softly he repeated: "You understand?"

"Sure," said Mazzioni's wife, slowly. She was no fool, and she was cottoning on. "Sure, I knew already."

Chang rang off, unhurriedly.

He was still worried and uneasy; he did not like having to work at speed like this, and did not like having to do so much himself. But it began to look as if the real emergency was past. If only he could find Estelle.

He left the hotel, and twenty minutes later, entered the café in Middle Street again. The plainclothes man he had shaken off was back on duty. Chang smiled at him politely, but didn't get a smile back.

In his office, Chang sat back, took another pinch of snuff, and glanced down at the figures in the book. It was silent again and he enjoyed the silence.

The telephone bell rang.

He lifted it and a man said: "This is Murphy."

Suddenly, Chang was acutely anxious; for Murphy never got in touch with him direct unless there was urgent news. Was this about Birdy Merrick or Estelle?

Had Estelle been found by the police? That was Chang's fear, that above all else.

Murphy was also an anxious man, although it took a great
deal to get on his nerves. Most days, he told his cronies
exactly what he thought of the police and how little they
mattered to him; and most days he meant exactly that. The
police had no terrors for him. He kept his nose clean, didn't
he? He had committed no crime of any kind in the past two
years except that of a little street corner betting, peddling
some bad liquor, which was hardly a crime at all, and—
inciting others to crime. No one named him as the insti-
gator, so that did not count.

Yet Murphy was edgy.

It was worse, because there had been a long, long spell of
freedom from fear. Everything had gone so smoothly that he
had become dangerously complacent. He had given more
orders himself than he should have done, instead of using
messengers, and he had gone to see Birdy.

He would not have told anyone in the world, but he was
frightened.

The sense of power which his habit of domination gave
him, had betrayed him. He should not have gone to Birdy's
house. Now, the Snide was in the hands of the police, and
the Snide had been seen to attack Birdy. It would be all
right if the police just handled Snide, but they might check
on everyone who had been after Birdy that day.

They were out in strength in the district.

Murphy had that nasty, sickening kind of feeling that the
police were out for a kill. It was Chang's doing. The orders
to get Birdy had come from Chang, even if they'd travelled
through three other people before reaching him. Murphy
did not propose to handle this with go-betweens, he wanted
to talk to Chang. There was the search for the red-haired
dancer, too, which had got nowhere, and was wasting men.

So he telephoned the Chinese.

Chang lifted the receiver, heard who it was, and then very
slowly shook his head. Murphy just reported, and asked if he
should keep up the search for B. and the skirt. Chang was
preparing to answer "for the skirt only," when there was an
interruption.

It was entirely coincidence that at that moment the door

burst open, but the sudden movement scared Chang, who actually jumped to his feet.

The door banged back.

Foster's sister came into the room with a scared-looking Chinese waiter behind her.

CHAPTER SIXTEEN

SANCTUARY?

CHANG looked up at Foster's sister. His eyes were lacklustre; his mouth was set in long, thin lines.

"Yes, proceed, please," he said into the telephone. "Now I must go." He rang off.

The woman had thrust her way past the waiter, outside, but Chang's expression stopped her, as a physical blow might do. She stood there, the sudden fear evident in her eyes, in the way her mouth opened and her teeth glinted. Behind her, the waiter hovered, hands rolling and rolling beneath his small white apron. Had Gideon seen the way he gazed at Chang, with silent supplication as to the Devil, Gideon would have hardened very much against Chang.

Then Chang spoke softly.

"Good evening, Mrs. Addinson. Please come in. Wen Li, please close the door." As the waiter obeyed and as Flo Addinson moved forward, Chang brought a smile from the depths of his self-discipline, then stood up and rounded the desk.

"Please sit down," he said. His voice was more sing-song than usual, as if he were fighting against showing his feelings. He touched the back of the easy chair and bowed. "Can I get you a drink?"

"No," she said. "No, thank you." She moved so that she could sit down. Chang bowed again and went back to his desk. Now the mask was on, but she had seen beneath it and she knew what was really there. When she had come in, she had been flushed, as with anger, actually with nervousness; now, she was very pale. Her eyes were bright, a shimmery kind of black, suggesting that she had a severe headache. She fumbled in her handbag, and Chang promptly stood up again and offered her cigarettes.

"Please smoke," he said.

She hesitated and then accepted a cigarette. He smiled as he flicked a lighter for her, but it was the smile of a robot. It was a genuine cigarette, too, there was no drug in it, yet the temptation to give her marihuana had been almost overwhelming.

She still wore the good black suit.

"Thank you."

"How can I help you, please?" murmured Chang.

"I came to—to ask you if you know what happened to my brother," she said.

He was outwardly almost back to normal, suave, almost solemn, spreading his hands.

"I was informed this morning of what had happened. Such a sad accident. I am very sorry."

"I'm not sure it was an accident," Flo Addinson said.

"Oh," said Chang, and his lips parted. Now he was in such complete command of himself that he folded his arms loosely across his narrow chest, and sat back in the chair. It was no indication of his feelings. "I do not understand you. He was run down by a car, is that not so? The driver did not stop."

Chang spread his hands.

"There are so many callous drivers——"

"Mr. Chang," the woman said steadily, "what association was there between my brother and you? Why did he see you so often? Why was he worried because of you?"

She had alarmed him, she knew; he could not hide it, even though he said:

"You are making mistakes, Mrs. Addinson, I cannot understand——"

"I must know what Eric had to do with you. The police kept asking me, they've followed me all day. Why is it? Do you know?"

Suavely, he insisted that he knew nothing, that he and her brother had just been acquaintances. But he questioned her tautly, trying to find out what she knew.

He learned little and soon she seemed tired.

"You have had a big shock," Chang murmured, when she rose to go. "Please allow me to send you home in my car,

Mrs. Addinson. It is no trouble. Unless you would like to stay to have dinner here? As my guest. I shall be very happy."

"No!" She jumped up. "No, thank you, I'd rather walk. If you're sure you can't help——"

"If I could, Mrs. Addinson, I would, gladly."

Chang pressed a bell, and the ringing sound could be heard faintly. In a moment, the door opened and the waiter appeared, big, flat, Mongolian face concealing his fear now.

"Show Mrs. Addinson downstairs," Chang said. He rounded the desk. "My very deep condolences, I assure you. I was very fond of Mr. Foster." He did not offer to shake hands, but bowed; and waited until the door closed on her.

Then he moved to his desk, swift as a flash, picked up a telephone, and was answered almost at once.

"The woman now downstairs," Chang said swiftly, "you will follow her and see if she is followed by the police. You understand?"

A man said, "Yes, sir."

Chang rang off. He didn't sit down, but went to the door and opened it. The music from the radiogram had started again, a fox-trot that sounded rather sensuous and slow. The landing light fell on Chang's black hair. He waited until the waiter came up the stairs, and the man with the flat Mongolian face could no longer hide his fear.

No one should have reached Chang's room without a warning preceding them; he had been panicked into forgetting to press a bell.

His feet dragged on the last two steps.

Chang waited until he was close to him, and then struck him across the face. The man swayed right and left under the impact of the savage blows, but didn't try to evade them. Chang did not speak, but turned back to his office. The waiter stumbled towards the narrow stairs. The fox-trot moaned on and the shuffling sound of dancing feet came clearly. Outside, a car horn tooted.

Outside, Flo Addinson walked towards Shaftesbury Avenue, was followed by a small man in a shabby suit, and by a plainclothes man detailed to follow her.

In his report to the Yard, this man said that Chang had had Mrs. Addinson followed almost to her door.

"You stay and keep an eye on her," he was ordered.

A few miles away from Soho, in a line which cut through the throbbing, cosmopolitan heart of the West End, through the dead City, and into the shadowy ill-lit streets of the East End, Murphy sat at a table in the front room of his house. For a man in his position, virtually boss of a powerful gang, he lived very humbly. The house was small, and the rooms tiny; only a twenty-inch television set, and bottles of every conceivable kind of drink standing on a cheap oak sideboard, suggested a man of means. That—and his wife. Murphy's wife wore real diamonds when she wore rings or jewellery at all, and she aped a refinement which, in this part of London, made her quite the lady.

She was watching the television and the light reflected from the screen shimmered on the engagement ring.

Murphy, a big, vague figure at the table, was looking at a small man who had only one arm; his left sleeve dangled empty by his side. The screen flickered, a man talked.

"That's right," Murphy said, "you tell 'em all to call it off, leave Birdy alone, see. And don't lose no time."

"Okay, but——"

"Scram," growled Murphy.

"Red," protested his wife, as if her mouth were full, "why don't you shut up or go in the other room?"

"You heard," Murphy said to the one-armed man.

"But Red——"

"Get out, I said."

Murphy got up from the table. The one-armed man hesitated, then went out. He closed the door softly. Murphy moved across to his wife's chair, which was placed immediately in front of the big television. She had a box of chocolates open at her side, and Murphy took one. Paper rustled. She put her hand over his, and squeezed. He whispered: "It's okay," and began to caress her. They watched the big screen, and listened to the deep voice coming from the set.

Meanwhile, the one-armed man sent the word round to call off the hunt.

What he had wanted to say was that just before he had been called in to Murphy, he'd been given a message saying that Ali and Lefty had cornered Birdy. It was next door to impossible to draw the hunt off in time.

Birdy did not find sanctuary in a ship, or in the docks, although he had run there believing that he could. A shadowy figure had appeared from behind some crates waiting for loading and turned him away.

Now he was back in his own native ground; in the narrow streets, among the towering warehouses, within sight of the silent river and the silent docks. Some kind of homing instinct had brought him here, after the sickening failure to get clear away on less familiar ground. He knew every inch of this, every hiding place, every hole and cellar; and he now tried to believe that he had more chance to save himself here.

He did not know if he was being closely watched.

He tried to persuade himself that this was his lucky night; the police car had saved him, he'd seen Lefty just in time, he'd beaten the Snide. But there was something else which filled him with terror. He'd left the Snide writhing in pain on the ground, where the police would pick him up. That would fill the others, especially Ali and Lefty, with a vindictive hatred.

He'd hurt one of the gang; in a way, had shopped him. Now it was more than a job for money, it was a vendetta.

In this narrow street it was very dark. That worried Birdy more than anything else. There should be a light on, jutting from a warehouse wall. Had it been broken? Had Ali put it out, so that he could confuse the hunted man?

Birdy moved furtively towards a corner. Round it, there was the ruin of a warehouse destroyed by fire; it was no use as a hiding-place because it was the first spot where the others would look. But beyond the warehouse was a church.

Birdy worked his way towards this.

He knew the church, as everyone did, but he had never been inside. He knew people who had; among them his daughter, before her death. He knew the elderly vicar whose chin was always on his chest as he walked about the parish, as if the dirt, the squalor, the crime, the vice, all the evil incarnate in man and so visible there, had weighed him down and sickened him, so that he served God only on sufferance and with a heavy heart. Birdy also knew the curate by sight, a spindly, unimpressive young man with a pointed nose, already a victim of catcalls and stink-bombs, a man likely to be led a hell of a life in his parish.

Birdy was very near the church. He had only to pass the ruins of the warehouse to reach it.

He had been hunted before but never like this, never to feel in deadly danger. That was why he saw the church as a very different thing; he saw it as a sanctuary, for no one would expect him to go there.

It offered him life and it was only a few yards away. The doors would be open as always. No ordinary criminal would go in and break open the offertory boxes, that was a crime which only perverts committed.

There was a yellow light at one window, at the far end of the church.

Birdy wondered who was there.

He reached the yawning entrance to the ruined warehouse, and, as he did so, a figure leapt at him.

It came from the warehouse; a dark figure with arms raised like a great bat. There was a sliding sound, a deadly rush of footsteps. Birdy knew that they had him; both of them were here. His terror seemed to explode inside him. *He screamed.*

He leapt forward and kicked against an outstretched leg and pitched forward. The fall drove the wind out of him. He banged his head so painfully that tears stung his eyes. He heard the thudding of his own heart, which was swelling and pounding with great fear. He saw pictures: Ethel, Murphy, Gideon, Ethel; *Ethel*.

He felt the sharp, searing pain of a razor cut in his cheeks; in one wrist.

He felt a man kneeling on his back, knee grinding into the vertebrae, agonizing, and enough to break his back. But he

couldn't think about that, only about razors and knives. He
tried to twist round but couldn't.

Suddenly, he felt the pressure relax.

That was only for a moment.

Lefty, the bottle artist, caught Birdy's right wrist, twisted
him, and turned him over so that he now lay on his back.
He stamped his heel into Birdy's stomach, so as to paralyse
him. Birdy felt hands at his wrists, pinioning him to the
ground. These hands belonged to Ali, and they were coming
for his face; his throat . . .

Unbelievably, the pressure at his wrist relaxed.

The awful thrust didn't come.

He heard other sounds, gasping, thudding, grunting. He
realized that men were fighting, and thought that the police
had come again. He rolled over but couldn't get up; his back
felt as if it had been broken.

He groaned and sobbed.

Then he heard the engine of a car, and although his eyes
were only open a fraction of an inch, saw the swaying beams
of headlamps. Had he been able to see properly, he would
also have seen Lefty reeling back against the warehouse wall,
and Ali and another man locked together, gasping and
struggling.

He did not recognize the spindly curate.

The police car screamed up, men jumped out, a door
slammed, a police whistle blew.

Every instinct Birdy had was to try to get away, but he
could not even roll over. He was vaguely aware of footsteps
and of a man running. Then came sharp, authoritative
voices; next, sharp metallic sounds—the click of handcuffs.
A man bent over him and the light of a torch fell into his face.

"Better get a doctor," said the man behind the torch.

"You take it easy, padre," said another man gruffly.
"I've radioed for an ambulance."

Birdy didn't know . . .

Lefty had escaped, but Ali was handcuffed and already
inside the police car. The ambulance was on the way. The
unhappy curate of the church had saved Birdy's life, and
risked his own; the news of that would spread, his stature

would rise; he might be hated but he had a chance to win respect.

Birdy just didn't know any of this.

He lost consciousness before the ambulance arrived, and while the policeman was giving him first aid for nasty cuts in his wrist and cheeks.

Gideon, looking solid, stolid and unimaginative, was still in the waiting-room with Lemaitre, but he knew that it was virtually a waste of time. Mazzioni had not said a word that mattered. Occasionally he said "no" to a leading question, but the main burden of what he had said was simple: he wanted a lawyer.

He'd been charged with complicity in the Waterloo raid, and had every right to legal representation.

The A.C., behind that window, might now have some idea of the frustration that the law itself created for the police. They had a man they were quite sure was guilty of a crime of violence and of highway robbery, and all they could do was ask him *questions*; there was no way to make him answer, no way to get past that silent, sullen front.

Then a sergeant came in.

"Can you spare a moment, Mr. Gideon?"

"Yes, what is it?"

"Outside, sir, if it's convenient."

"All right," Gideon said. He looked at Mazzioni, who was sneering up into his face. The Italian's fingers were stained dark brown with nicotine, but he hadn't tried to take out cigarettes, and Gideon hadn't offered him one. Gideon had an intuitive feeling that he was looking at someone really evil; one who could kill and maim remorselessly, who seemed to have no redeeming feature. Nothing in Mazzioni's manner suggested that he was worth a moment's compunction; or a cigarette.

Gideon went out.

The A.C. was coming out of the room from which he had been watching, and the sergeant glanced at him, then back at Gideon.

"Sorry to interrupt, sir, but there's a Mr. Ledbetter at the main hall, asking for—er—Mr. Mazzioni. He asked whether it's true that Mazzioni is on a charge, and insisted on seeing you personally, sir."

Gideon echoed: "*Ledbetter.*"

"Yes, sir."

"Hmm," said Gideon heavily. "All right, tell him I'll see him in a few minutes." He waited for the man to walk briskly along the corridor. "Well, they didn't lose much time, did they?"

"Who?" asked the A.C.

"Ledbetter's already done two jobs for Chang, or friends of Chang," Gideon said. "I don't trust him an inch. Hard to say why. Good solicitor, done some first-class work, until a year or two ago there was nothing rumoured against him, but now—how did he get to know about the arrest, unless Mazzioni has friends who passed it on? That's what I'd like to know more than anything else. *How* did Ledbetter get to know?"

The A.C. didn't speak.

"Can't stop him from seeing the Italian," Gideon went on gloomily. "I could stall, but it'd be a waste of time. Better let them meet. There ought," added Gideon with feeling, "to be a law against allowing accused and his solicitor to have a *tête-à-tête.*"

He looked and sounded tired and disappointed.

He was much more disappointed, twenty minutes later, when he heard about the "alibi". More; he was angry, feeling quite sure that the alibi was faked. He sensed a hidden nervousness in Ledbetter's manner, too.

He could have used an alternative charge, of being in unlawful possession of dangerous drugs, but he didn't; he could hold it over Mazzioni's head, and it might help in the next day or two. Mazzioni "cleared" of the mail van job was better free to meet his cronies than on a charge.

Gideon tried to bluff by holding the Italian for the night.

"I take the strongest exception to that," Ledbetter said decisively. "There is nothing to prevent you from asking the witness whether she can offer supporting evidence, and if she can, then it's up to you to check it at once. My client was miles away at the time of the crime you've charged him with. I'm sorry you've made a mistake, but I'm more sorry for my client than I am for you."

Gideon looked at him thoughtfully.

"I don't know whom I'm most sorry for," he said. "Yet."

Ledbetter coloured . . .

When he and Mazzioni had gone, the A.C. looked in on Gideon, approved the decision to hold over the dangerous drugs charge, and asked:

"Think you can make Mazzioni crack in time?"

"Dunno," said Gideon frankly. "More than anything else, I want that dancer, Estelle."

"Any news?"

"Not yet," Gideon said.

The A.C. went off as glum as Gideon, and Gideon sat back and studied transcripts of Mazzioni's statements, and the record of the woman who'd given him an alibi. He wanted to talk to her, but——

Before he could even think about visiting her, he had to check what reports were coming in. He hadn't yet heard about the night's biggest job, at the Mid-Union Safe Deposit in the City.

CHAPTER SEVENTEEN

THE BIGGEST JOB . . .

EVERY part of London had known its moments of crisis that night, every Division received its urgent call for help. The placid men in the Information Room had taken call after call to 999 without fuss, quietly reassuring agitated callers, extracting the necessary information, passing it through to the Flying Squad, the Patrol Cars or the Divisions for action.

The Yard seemed more alive by night than by day.

The reports were on Gideon's desk, in a thick sheaf of notes written in a bold, legible hand and a welcome economy of phrase; and the sergeant stood looking at Gideon as if he hoped the Superintendent would make a favourable comment.

There were the burglaries; dozens of them. Attacks on women alone in the streets, smash-and-grab jobs, two club raids with fifty-seven names taken. Great Marlborough Street was overflowing with the so-called flower of the aristocracy, most of whom took a raid on a gambling club for a joke, or pretended to.

There was the inevitable crop of charges of soliciting, there were two men accused of attempting to murder their wives. One was still belligerent after being stopped from thrashing his wife, the other cowed and frightened, so much so that it was hard to believe that he had ever been brandishing a knife, as if ready to kill.

Three men had been picked up in the Occidental Hotel for passing sludge, or forged money. A man who had already served two sentences for fraud was held on suspicion of trying to earn his third sentence; crimes of all kinds and all varieties were committed in the few hours that were left of Gideon's day, but there was only one which held dynamite.

The note read: *City Police glad if you will call them, suspected burglary Mid-Union Safe Deposit.*

"Oh ho," grunted Gideon.

He skimmed through the other notes, and then the telephone bell rang. The sergeant could have answered it, but Gideon's hand was already on the smooth black surface.

"Gideon here."

He listened.

"Are you *sure*?" His voice rose, his face brightened.

"Oh, that's fine," he said. "How badly hurt? . . . Well, he'll get over it. Tell his wife, won't you?" He rang off and looked up at the door as it opened, and Lemaitre came in, very subdued. "Thought you'd gone home," he said.

"Daren't," said Lemaitre gloomily.

Gideon chuckled.

"What's pleased you?" demanded Lemaitre. "The last I saw of you, you looked——"

"They've picked up Birdy."

"That so?" Lemaitre brightened. "Okay?"

"Cuts on his right wrist and his cheeks and some nasty bruising on his back and stomach, but an X-ray showed nothing to worry about," said Gideon. "They got Ali, too."

"You mean that little lascar swine?"

"He's being held—was caught with the knife on him and in the act of using it. Actually a curate over there stopped it, young chap who's new to the district."

Lemaitre whistled.

"If he hadn't been new, he wouldn't have interfered! Ali would have knifed him as soon as look at him. That's a bit better, anyhow. We've still got the chance of getting somewhere through the Snide and Ali. One of them will probably squeal, and if we could tuck Murphy away for a few years it would be something. What do you think of that crook, Led——"

"Okay, sergeant," Gideon interrupted, "I'll call you when I want you. Thanks—very good job."

"Thank you, sir." The sergeant hurried out.

"Hell, what would it have mattered if I had told him what

I thought of Ledbetter?" growled Lemaitre. "And to think what I've done for this night's work—proper mucked things up with Fifi. If you'd seen the way she looked when I told her I had to stand her up."

"Go home, wake her up, and tell her you love her," said Gideon, "and blame me for standing her up."

"Strewth!" exclaimed Lemaitre, "it's bad enough when I wake her if I just get home late. Anything much in?"

"The City chaps want me," said Gideon. "Some trouble at the Mid-Union Safe Deposit. Better call them." He stifled a yawn. "And then come hell or high water, I'm going *home*."

He felt flat again as he spoke. The temporary stimulant of the news about Birdy had faded in fresh gloom about Mazzioni. Ledbetter's part depressed him, too; there were plenty of unreliable solicitors, but they didn't grow on trees. Few of them were crooked for the sake of it, usually they drifted, some were blackmailed.

"I wouldn't mind a bit of action," Lemaitre said. "Got anything?"

He really funked going home.

"Go and see this woman," Gideon said, and tapped the card with the name and address of Mazzioni's "alibi". "Try to shake her about where she was and who she was with this afternoon."

"Oke," Lemaitre promised.

Gideon called the City Police.

Earlier in the evening, the night staff of the Mid-Union Safe Deposit Company had settled down to the usual quiet night's work. Most of this would be keeping records. There would be some business in the early hours of the morning, when the really sensible, who had taken out jewels for wear, brought them back instead of taking them home. That "rush" would last for an hour, and after it there would be nothing until the morning staff took over. Only three men were on duty; a fourth, usually present, was on sick-leave.

Three could cope.

The building of the Mid-Union Safe Deposit Company was a large stone-faced one, in narrow Wattle Street, and was sandwiched between a block of offices let to a hundred different firms—from lawyers to tea brokers, rubber merchants to shipping companies, accountants and insurance brokers—and the Head offices of one of the largest insurance companies. Mid-Union actually owned the building, but let off the ground and upper floors, retaining a basement office and two big vaults, each below basement level. The entrance was through Wattle Street and past a wide doorway which was protected, when necessary, by a strong steel door.

This was always open.

No one could step through the doorway without sending two warnings through to the officials on the floor below; one warning was electric, the other was by secret ray; neither rang a bell, but each flashed a light which would be seen at once by the men on duty.

These were behind a strong grille, heavily protected, and entrance could be gained only through a small doorway which was kept locked and unlocked for every fresh customer. No customer was allowed in the vaults by himself—neither the one at first level, where the more frequently needed deposits were stored, nor the deep vault. An armed official always accompanied him. By night, it was sometimes necessary to keep customers waiting, but if they wished they could drop their packets into a night safe—much on the bank system—and this would be put in a community safe until they came to put it in their own box.

The staff took the daily and nightly handling of valuables for granted. On really busy days, a million pounds' worth of precious stones would be brought in or taken out, and no one thought twice about it.

Except Fitzroy . . .

About the time that Gideon had finished his dinner, one of the three members of the staff had gone into the bottom vaults, to check some entries. That was regular enough, and he should be gone for about half an hour. In fact, he was longer. Neither of the others was worried about this, for some jobs were difficult to estimate.

All the men on duty carried guns, but in the forty-nine years of its existence, the Mid-Union had never had an attempted robbery. This did not make anyone careless; the warning system was perfect, and each night-duty official was trained in the use of his gun. They were selected men with brilliant war records. No one over forty-five was employed by night.

The big general office behind the reception desk was empty by night, too.

When the first man had been gone for forty minutes—by then, Gideon had seen Ledbetter—one of the others went to look for him, leaving only the night-manager behind the grille.

The second man didn't come back either.

The night-manager, a youthful forty-one, knew his staff well and was quite sure that they were reliable. He was going to find out what was keeping them, when two customers came in. Both were men, both wanted to deposit jewels. They were regular customers, the night-manager could not offend them, and he took them downstairs to the first vault, one at a time.

In all, that job took him twelve minutes.

He locked the reception desk door on the two customers, and hurried to the narrow stone steps which led to the lower vault.

Half-way down, he stopped.

Ought he to telephone the police, and make sure that if anything were wrong——

It was too late.

A man appeared at the foot of the steps, holding an automatic pistol. The night-manager felt as if death had suddenly knocked loudly at his door. The man with the gun was masked, tall, lean, leathery-looking. The gun was very steady. He started up the stairs and the manager backed a step, but didn't move far. He was in between two alarm bells that would call the police, and his only hope of getting to one was to turn and rush up the steps.

The eyes of Fitzroy, the man with the gun, discouraged notions of heroism.

"Take it easy," Fitzroy said. "You won't get hurt if you do what you're told, but if you try any tricks, you'll get hurt badly. *And* you might not recover."

The manager licked his lips.

Fitzroy was within two yards of him.

If he jumped——

He jumped.

As he moved, he had an awful sense of failure, of doom. He saw the gunman draw to one side, saw a long leg shoot out. He could not avoid it and fell headlong down the stairs.

Another masked man appeared at the foot of them and picked him up. Dazed and bruised, he could only think of the gun.

Fitzroy spoke brightly:

"Just do what you're told, and you won't get hurt. Let's have your keys for a start."

"No. No, I——"

The second man struck the manager sharply across the face and spun him round. The keys were fastened to a thick leather belt running round his waist. The second man used a pair of wire-cutters to cut the belt, then pushed the manager towards the lower vault. The manager was too frightened to think clearly, but a thought flashed into his mind.

These men seemed to know their way about.

Entrance must have been forced from *below*. That wasn't possible, it——

He was pushed into the large bottom vault, where big, solid safes and rows of metal boxes lined the walls from floor to ceiling. On the floor, lying on their backs, were the two clerks. In one wall was a hole nearly two feet square, and by it was a heap of dirt and debris, chippings of cement, everything to show how the "impossible" had been achieved.

Then a man thrust a cloth over the manager's head, tied it at the back, seized his hands and bound them, and then laid him down.

He did not know what was happening; all he knew was that he was alive. Fitzroy looked at him and grinned, then turned to the two men with him, pulling off his mask.

"I'm going up to the office to look after the customers." He chuckled again. "They won't know how safe their baubles are!" He went off, moving easily and outwardly confident, and he whistled softly as he took the place of the manager.

The odds had been nicely calculated.

He knew that the fourth member of the night staff was away. He knew that the hour for late deposits was almost past, and that even if there were more, they would only be for the upper floor. He could lock himself in with the depositor, see the goods put in the box, and wish the man "good night". His two assistants were expert safebreakers, and if they managed to open only two of the safes and two or three dozen of the metal boxes, the haul would be sensational. So he whistled as he sat at the desk, and made a show of working when he heard footsteps.

A young man came down and stopped short at sight of him.

"Evening, sir," said Fitzroy, getting up.

"Good evening. Isn't Mr. Ilott here?"

"Downstairs at the moment," said Fitzroy glibly, "but I can send for him if you really want him."

"Well——"

"Or I can help you, sir." Fitzroy looked so brisk and friendly, smiled so amiably, and spoke with such conviction, that the depositor gave way. He had his own key. Fitzroy let him into the upper deposit vault, escorted him to his box, and watched him deposit a diamond ring and two diamond drop earrings.

"I always feel safer when they're locked away," said the depositor.

"I bet you do," said Fitzroy warmly. "I would if they were mine, too. I'll tell Mr. Ilott that you've been, sir."

"Thanks," the depositor said, and left with a hearty "Good night".

Fitzroy went back to his desk, and whistled under his breath until the man's footsteps had faded; then he lit a cigarette, and took out a newspaper folded to the crossword puzzle. Now and again he perked his head up, and listened; he had heard imagined sounds from the street.

Down below, the others were working quickly and with great skill.

Two safes were open, and cash, diamonds, jewellery of all kinds and a little bullion, were loaded into canvas mail van sacks. One man was working at a third safe, the other was beginning on the steel boxes. He had a tool which pierced them at the edges, and, working rather like wire cutters or tin openers, tore a big hole. He made some noise, but it did not travel even up the narrow stone steps to Fitzroy.

He opened box after box.

The other man forced the door of his third safe, and, hardly troubling to examine the jewellery in it, dropped it into another sack.

The first man had emptied twenty-one boxes.

"About all we can manage," he said, looking round the vault regretfully. "I hope we haven't missed any juicy ones. They could tell us!" He grinned across at the three prisoners, but didn't go towards them.

He went up to the main floor, and, without showing himself in the office, whispered:

"You there, Fitz?"

Fitz called immediately: "Yes."

"We're going."

"Nice haul?"

"Plenty." There was an echo of satisfaction in the man's voice; an echo of excitement, too. Fitzroy got up and went to the head of the stairs, leaving the reception desk untenanted for a moment. He was pulling at a cigarette, and excitement showed in the brightness of his eyes; the other man showed his with a slight quiver of the lips and the hands. "Wouldn't like to guess how much, but not less than a couple of hundred thousand."

"*Nice* work! Off you go."

"How long will you stay?"

"Ten minutes," said Fitzroy, "and then I'll lock the front doors, and any customers will be annoyed!" The shrillness of his laugh was another betrayal of his taut nerves.

He went back to the reception desk. He didn't hear a car stop outside, but for some reason went suddenly tense.

Below, his companions were taking the loot out through the hole they had made.

A man and woman came hurrying down the steps, the man in evening dress, the woman wearing a long dress and a mink wrap. The man produced his key and his card, and said briskly:

"Don't want to rush you, but I'm in a hurry."

"All right," said Fitzroy. "I'll be as quick as I can."

There was no reason at all why they should suspect that anything was wrong; no reason for them to believe that anything was. They looked natural, happy. The woman was little more than a girl, and she had a glow in her eyes which suggested that she was not used to hanging on to this particular arm.

Number 413—close to the head of the stairs leading to the lower vault.

Fitzroy, all right until then, became slow-moving, in spite of the impatience of the man; he was drawing attention to himself by his slowness.

He unlocked the door. He knew that it was a matter of custom for the depositor to come in alone, but the girl was like a limpet. A brunette, rather nice, low-bosomed dress, everything. Fitzroy looked at her and swallowed hard. This was where he could easily make a fool of himself.

He forced a smile.

"Depositor only, please."

"Won't be a jiff, dear," said the young man, and prised himself free.

Fitzroy's fists, clenched until then, unclenched as he closed and locked the door. It seemed a very long way to Number 413, and it seemed as if the man had eyes that could see through the brick walls. Fitzroy's body was a-quiver, it was a good thing that the depositor had to unlock his own box.

He did so, took out a string of pearls, left everything else in, locked the box again, and was back at the grille ahead of

Fitzroy. Fitzroy breathed rather hissingly. It was over and he'd kept his head.

After that it was easy.

He did not give a thought to the three prisoners.

It did not occur to him that trouble might lie ahead.

CHAPTER EIGHTEEN

THE TUNNEL

GIDEON heard the voice of the City Superintendent, warm and friendly, broad in its Scots accent. Gideon was not thinking deeply about this call yet, for he was still preoccupied, although beginning to warn himself that he must go home and get some rest. Only the countless loose ends which came at the very end of every day were left undone.

"Hallo, Alec," he said, "what can I do for you?"

"George, man, I'm puzzled a wee bit," the Superintendent said. "You know the Mid-Union place? They keep half the valuables of London there, which is a slight exaggeration but you know what I mean."

"I ken," said Gideon, straight-faced.

"Stop your joking, man. One of the regular customers went there a while ago and said that he didn't recognize the official at the reception desk. The official seemed to know his way about all right, but he didn't have anyone with him. And that's a curious thing, George, under the regulations there are always two men on duty at the desk. I've never known it any different. So I told my man to keep a sharp look-out, and just this minute he's telephoned to say that the doors are locked. Now that's not done any night in the year, the Mid-Union is always open. So I'm putting a cordon round the place. I thought you'd like to know."

Gideon said very slowly: "Thanks, Alec, that's good of you." He was thinking more deeply now; worriedly. The City man had probably exaggerated, but the valuables in that safe deposit were worth a fabulous sum. The City police did not want to handle it on their own, and hadn't lost any time asking for help. "All right, I'll put word round and have some support sent along." Gideon went on: "Are you going there yourself?"

"Aye, I think so."

"I'll see you there," promised Gideon.

He still did not, could not, understand how important the job was; but it might be very big indeed. The drive to Wattle Street in the night air would wake him up a bit. If this fizzled out, he could go straight home.

"Lem, hand everything over to Cartwright, will you?" he said. "And then go home. Better forget Estelle, she'll have to keep till morning. Take a chance on getting kicked out of bed."

Lemaitre grimaced and moved to his telephone.

Gideon went out.

He was in the curiously unsatisfied mood. He could not really complain about the day, and the capture of Sayer had been of first importance. A lot had gone right, too. At heart, he knew that two things had gone very deep: the discovery of Foster's duplicity, and his death; and the face of Mrs. Saparelli. These made the finding of Estelle more urgent, but it would all take time. There were the drugs at Mazzioni's, too—the Italian didn't know they'd been found. He'd probably make a slip——

Gideon telephoned orders to the Flying Squad C.O. to have all available squad cars concentrated on the City area, and then hurried out. Few policemen were about. A squad car was waiting ready for an emergency call, with two men sitting in front. His own car shone darkly under a lamp immediately above it.

Big Ben boomed eleven.

Gideon got into the Wolseley, slammed the door, and then, for some reason, remembered Kate. There was an added cause for his discontent. He could picture her running down the stairs to him, almost eagerly. *Eagerly.* He could picture her bright eyes and attractive face as she had sat next to him on the way to Oxford Street, and the jaunty grace of her walk as she had left him. She hadn't looked back. She'd obviously been pleased that he had taken the trouble to drop in, and to give her the lift. It would have been all right had he been able to go home early, but here it was eleven o'clock, and even if this turned out to be a false alarm, it would be midnight before he was home.

He didn't hurry.

Two squad cars passed him, on their way to the City.

Fitzroy finished locking the door at the top of the narrow steps, and, still whistling, hurried down them to the brightly-lit reception desk. The street door was closed and they were safe. He opened a drawer and found some loose change and a few one pound and ten shilling notes. He stuffed these into his pocket, saluted the drawer, and then looked round quickly, making sure that he hadn't left anything behind. The stubs of three cigarettes were in an ash-tray; he emptied this into a piece of paper, screwed it up, and thrust it into his pocket.

Whistling, he went down the next flight of steps to the main deposit room. The three prisoners lay stretched out, and one of them was wriggling.

"You'll soon feel better, chum, don't worry," Fitzroy said, and then hurried towards the lower vault and the hole in the wall.

He saw one of the others coming back into the vault, *out* of the hole. The man was treading on bits of cement and dirt.

When he saw this, Fitzroy stood stock still and open-mouthed. No shock could have been greater. He had pictured his accomplices already driving through London to the safety of obscurity. It was like seeing the ghost of a living man. But this was no ghost; it was a youth in the early twenties, looking badly scared.

"What the hell's this?" Fitzroy demanded in a squeaky voice.

"We—we can't get out," the man said, as thinly.

Fitzroy just would not believe it.

"Don't talk a lot of bull! We can——"

"Police are—are in Hay Court," the man announced.

Fitzroy didn't speak.

The light was good and he had not put on his mask again. He had pleasant features, an open face, and smiling blue eyes; only they were not smiling now. A new light came into them, cold and ugly.

"We've got to get out," he said. "Where's Jem?"

"Keeping watch."

"Come on," said Fitzroy.

He had to bend almost double, to get through the hole. He took a torch out of his pocket, and it showed the gap they had made in days of patient labour. Now they made grating noises as they moved along, and once or twice Fitzroy bumped his head painfully on the uneven roof; but he didn't stop. Soon, bright light glowed.

He reached the cellar of the building next door, one used for storing old files and documents. The night watchman of the building was in his, Fitzroy's, pay; he did not know what they were doing in the cellar, just turned a blind eye and did not come beyond the first cellar level.

The steps leading to that cellar were of stone, crumbling away. Fitzroy went up them slowly. He moved with great caution, while the full significance of what was happening gradually caught up with him.

He reached the ground floor.

There were two ways out of this building; the big, massive front door, which was barred and bolted to prevent anyone from coming in; and a small doorway at the back, leading to a little courtyard and, by a narrow alley, to Milchester Street. It should have been so easy. The only problem was to get the sacks through the alley to the small car which was parked nearby, in a little private parking place. They had studied the time of the police patrols in the district, and had judged the right moment.

Fitzroy went through the deserted building, his footsteps making little sound on the stone floor of the hall; then on linoleum over wide boards; finally over tiles. Soon, he saw the faint light against a window. He could not make out the figure of the third burglar, Jem, but heard the faint whisper.

"How many outside?"

"Dunno."

Fitzroy moved towards the window. He shone his torch so that the beam fell upon a chair which he knew one of the others had put into position. He climbed up, and could now peer through a window into the courtyard.

He saw *three* uniformed policemen.

He got down. His heart was thumping, but he told himself that he wasn't really frightened. He had been in tough spots before, and had got out of them. He slid his right hand into his hip pocket; the steel of an automatic pistol felt very cold.

"How many in Wattle Street?"

"Several," Jem muttered. He was the tallest of the three. "Tell you what——"

"What?"

"We could go up the first floor, and climb up, then——"

"Carrying what?" Fitzroy asked sneeringly.

Jem didn't answer.

"We've got a fortune," Fitzroy said, "and we're going to keep it. Stay here a minute."

He turned back towards the front entrance. He would not have admitted it to anyone, but he did not really know what to do. He had been so sure that this way of escape would be left open, because it didn't affect Mid-Union. He began to ask himself what had gone wrong, but gave that up as futile. He could see the street lights showing against the huge fanlight, but if he went into one of the offices . . .

He tried a door handle; and the door opened.

He stepped into an office. This had frosted glass halfway up the window, but through the top he could see the dark shape of a lamp standard; as he went in, the light outside grew brighter and the engine of a car sounded. The car swept along the street, the driver changed gear and turned a corner.

A desk stood close to the window.

Fitzroy climbed up and peered cautiously over the frosted glass into the street.

Two cars were parked a little way along. Men in uniform and in plainclothes were outside the entrance to the Mid-Union Building. It wasn't surprising that the police should concentrate on that, but——

How could he get out?

He climbed down and went away from the window as another car arrived and stopped.

He began to sweat.

They had to get out, now. If the police forced their way into the building next door, they would find the hole in five minutes, would be in this building in ten; squeezed between the two forces, Fitzroy and his companions wouldn't have a chance.

"Jem," he said, when back in the rear hall.

"Yes?"

"Any reinforcements out there?"

"No."

"Okay. I'm going to open the door. I'll keep them busy. I'll take a few sparklers with me, that'll fool them. I'll draw them off and when I've done that, you two get to the car. Take a sack each and make it snappy."

"But——"

"Think of anything better?" Fitzroy demanded angrily.

"No, but——"

"Then quit crabbing."

"Fitz," the other man said, in a whisper which was hardly audible, "you won't go killing——"

"Who said anything about killing?"

"That gun?"

"What a gutless pair to work with," Fitzroy growled. "Okay, if you want to spend the next ten years in jail, I don't. Do it my way." He didn't give them a chance to answer, but went to the door.

He heard one of them breathing very heavily, then heard the rustle as he picked up the bag.

He opened the door a fraction, mildly surprised that it did open. He knew that the police would be watching intently, and that they hoped that whoever was inside would come out without realizing that anyone was lying in wait.

The light shone on the paving stones of the courtyard; on the frosted glass of the window of offices surrounding it; on a grating; on a drain pipe down which water gurgled. Apart from that there was no sound.

He opened the door wider.

He saw nothing.

He called in a whisper: "Looks as if they've gone." At heart he did not believe that, but he was desperately anxious to get away, and wishful thinking fooled him for a few dazzling seconds. "Come on."

He stepped into the courtyard.

No one was in sight and there were no shadows. Somewhere, high up, the wind whistled, but in this yard all was still. Perhaps they hadn't realized that the door was opening. Perhaps they had gone to reinforce men at the Mid-Union building, not this.

He tiptoed across the courtyard to the end of the alley.

The others were in the courtyard now.

He carried the gun in front of him, but with the passing of every second, the palpitations grew less, for the chances of success were obviously greater. The car wasn't far away, he would lead the way to it, and keep cover while they got in.

Then he heard a gasp:

"Fitz!" a man cried.

Fitzroy spun round, saw one of his accomplices stagger, and saw a policeman jumping *down* from a window just above the door.

Other police appeared at first floor windows, a whistle shrilled out along the alley.

Fitzroy fired at the falling policeman, did not wait to see if he had scored a hit, but turned towards the alley and ran. All hope of loot was gone, escape was his one purpose— escape, with the determination to shoot himself to safety.

CHAPTER NINETEEN

THE ESCAPE

GIDEON reached the offices of the Mid-Union Company when two police cars and a small crowd of policemen were outside. He slowed down and a uniformed man wearing the helmet of the City Police came forward, recognized him, and said:

"Superintendent Cameron's in Hay Court, sir."

"Hay Court? Where—oh, I know. Thanks. All quiet?"

"Someone inside there as shouldn't be," the constable said emphatically. "The manager's on the way with another set of keys."

"Good," said Gideon. "Thanks." He drove on, not travelling fast, looking for the narrow turning which would take him to Hay Court. He knew the City almost as well as he knew his own Square Mile, but not quite as well. In the West End he could have found his way about blindfolded; here, he wasn't sure, until he saw another tall City policeman at a corner. The man put out an arm to stop the car; a silent, immutable force, showing all the confidence in the world.

Gideon poked his head through the window.

"I'm Gideon. Is Superintendent Cameron here?"

"Just along here, sir, but I shouldn't take the car if I were you. We've put a barricade up."

"Oh. Thanks. I'll park along here." Gideon drove on a few yards and climbed out.

The night air was fresh but by no means cold. The sky had a clearness and the stars a brightness which were more common to Winter than to Spring. Gideon felt not so much tired now as relaxed.

He walked briskly and with hardly a sound towards Hay Court. At the end of this narrow, cobbled road, he saw a row of galvanized dustbins beneath a gas light and grinned at the form of the barricade. Two policemen stood on duty, one peered at and recognized him and saluted. Gideon passed between two dustbins, unpleasantly aware of the smell of rotting vegetables.

There was a small square, surrounded by high buildings, and with two recesses holding the doorways to small buildings, and one lane, which led towards Fenchurch Street. He remembered it well now. He saw two policemen climbing up the side of one office building and watched them in the semi-darkness. They were making for a window sill above a door which was closed, and edged their way along.

He saw shadowy figures at one of the windows.

Cameron came up.

"Hallo, George," he greeted, "good to see you." They shook hands. Cameron was a man of medium size; even in this light his fair features and sharp, pointed nose were evident. "We think they'll come out this way, a door opened a few minutes ago. And there's a car waiting not far away, often parked there late, I'm told."

"Any idea who it is?"

"No." Cameron whispered a few other details: that he had telephoned the manager of the Mid-Union Company and been told that the top gates should not be locked. An observant constable had really started this, and a puzzled customer taken it a step further.

Cameron was in a mood for rejoicing; so was Gideon. Usually they were called after the job was done, when the men and the loot were miles away, and the whole resources of the Force had to be called on, straining the men almost beyond endurance. This should be a short, sharp case, and——

"Look!" whispered Cameron.

In the faint light they saw the doorway open. Then a man appeared and looked round cautiously. Had he looked up, he must have seen the policemen poised above him. He hesitated, then went back into the building.

Gideon's big hand closed round Cameron's arm, and gave a silent message. Cameron breathed:

"*Aye, a gun.*"

Gideon felt his mood changing to one of acute wariness. He wanted to shout a warning to everyone else within earshot, but dare not. He sensed Cameron's increased tension. Then the man with the gun came forward, other dark figures emerged from the doorway.

One of the policemen jumped.

The movement, the gasp and the scuffle of footsteps came quickly and then the first man swung round, and Gideon saw him raise his arm.

"*Look out!*" roared Gideon.

But the shot came before his words. He saw the policeman falling and heard a kind of squeal. Then the men who had come from the doorway all moved together, but it was impossible to tell one from another. A heavy weight fell. Policemen closed with one man, and then torch lights shone out, carving Hay Court into sections of bright light and darkness, showing the pallor of frightened faces, the darkness of clothes, the gun, struggling feet, a big sack.

Gideon concentrated on the gunman.

Fitzroy was free of police for a split second, but another was running at him, and Cameron moved, too. Fitzroy fired, point-blank.

". . . . swine," Gideon muttered under his breath.

He waited, like a footballer ready to go into the tackle, swaying from side to side. The policeman fell back, then crumpled up.

Fitzroy was free of him—and Fitzroy saw another policeman coming at him.

He fired again.

The policeman swayed to one side, and Fitzroy made a wild leap, passed him, and reached the end of the alley. The gun was waving as he ran.

Only one big man in plainclothes was in his path.

"Now, drop that," Gideon said. He was surprised that his own voice was level and intelligible. "Don't be a fool."

For a second, a long, frightening, deathly second, neither man moved.

Gideon knew that words were useless, only one thing would save him.

He plunged forward, hands outstretched to clutch the gunman's ankles. It was impossible to tell whether the other would shoot at him or not; if he pointed the gun downwards and fired, he couldn't miss.

Gideon felt the cloth of the man's trousers in his fingers. He tried to grab the ankles, but missed. A foot cracked against his temple, and there was an explosive sound inside his head; he wasn't sure whether it came from a shot or the kick. He drew his hands in instinctively to protect his head. The thief jumped over him and the sharp crack of another shot came.

Gideon began to pick himself up drunkenly.

No one came to help him.

He got to one knee. There was a nasty throbbing in his ears, but he knew that he hadn't been shot, because there was no blood. He felt light-headed. Sounds came as if from a long way off. On his feet, he staggered until he came up against the wall.

Someone said: "You all right, sir?"

"Yes. Yes, don't worry about——" he didn't finish, but tried to focus his gaze. The light in the court was brighter and clearer now, coming from rooms in the nearby offices as well as the torches. It was a strange, almost a frightening sight. Men bent over two policemen who lay on the ground, one of them grunting, moaning. Two men, each handcuffed to a policeman, were standing quite still. Sacks near the doorway told their own story.

Then, from some way off, came the bark of another shot.

"I've got a nasty feeling," Gideon said, "that that brute's going to get away."

"You all right, George?" Cameron demanded.

"Yes, thanks."

"What've you done to your head?"

"Just a kick."

"We'll get him," Cameron said, "we'll get him if——"

He didn't finish. Words were futile, rage with himself as well as with the prisoner who had escaped was just as futile.

The simple truth was that the man had shot his way out of
the ambush and, in doing so, wounded three policemen, one
of whom seemed to be in a bad way.

Ambulances had been summoned.

A general call had gone out for the gunman, and at least
they knew his name and had a description; one of the prisoners had talked freely; words had spilled out with fear.

It had all happened ten minutes ago and it seemed like
hours. Gideon, his head aching but no longer giddy, had
sent out the instructions by radio-telephone, but he felt sick.
It wasn't because of the kick or the fall—it was because of
the failure.

Could one call it failure?

Already he was beginning to ask himself questions about
it and his own part in it. Cameron had been in charge, but
he needn't have left so much to the City man. The truth was
that he had taken this too casually, almost like an exercise;
"trapped men cannot get away" had been his axiom, and he
hadn't allowed for a killer shooting his way to freedom.
Failure as such wasn't the only bad thing. It meant that the
Yard and all the Divisions would have to screw themselves up
to a high-powered effort, and tension was never-ending.
If all three men had been captured, the police could have
breathed more easily; only routine jobs need have worried
them, jobs like this seldom came up more than once in two
or three weeks.

Well, it had to be done.

The night duty man at the Yard would be doing much
the same as he had been doing all day, every policeman in
London would be steeling himself. Gideon couldn't explain why, but it was a fact that if a policeman were shot and
injured, especially if one were killed, something seemed to be
infused into the rest of the Force. They became killer-
minded. They would work until they dropped and they
would get this man, Fitzroy. But that wasn't the beginning
or the end. They could only do one job at a time, and the
little crooks who worked by night were quick to sense when
the police had a big job on. This was a night when the
graph of London's crime would shoot upwards sharply. In

temporary, perhaps in false security, the sneak-thieves would be out like vultures ready to peck and tear at an unprotected carcase.

Gideon knew all this.

He knew, too, that if he had grabbed an inch closer to the gunman's ankles, he would have brought the man down, and there would have been no need for the great hunt. That was one cause of his bitterness. He of all men knew how tightly the police were stretched; and he could have eased the burden for a little while, but had failed.

There it was.

He heard a bell ringing, shrilly; an ambulance was on its way. In the distance, another sounded. Then men came from Wattle Street. Next Gideon and Cameron went through the building next to Mid-Union, and found the hole which had been made into the lower vault.

Gideon's lips turned down.

"They didn't do that in a hurry," he said.

"Dunno," said Cameron, and bent down to pick up a small electric drill. "Home-made job and it wouldn't make much noise." He paused. "You can't get through there, can you?"

"No," said Gideon.

"See you the other side." Cameron was already on his knees, ready to climb through.

Gideon walked back into Hay Court, along the narrow cobbled road into Wattle Street. The door was being unlocked, policemen were waiting warily, in case other gunmen lay in wait. None did. Gideon and a scared, worried manager who had hurried from his home in Hampstead, led the way down the stairs. The empty reception office, the narrow stairs, the ordinary strong-room—and the three members of the staff were found, stretched out, two of them struggling with their bonds, the other unconscious.

Outside, the hunt for Fitzroy went on.

Gideon yawned.

It was half-past twelve, exactly fifteen hours since he had stepped into his office that morning, an age ago. He was by himself for a few minutes, sitting in his car. No word had come in of Fitzroy's capture and the hunt might go on for days. The ambulances had carried off the wounded police-men and one of the Mid-Union staff, who was suffering badly from shock and fright. None of the victims was likely to die: that was one relief. The accomplices had told their story without defiance, as if they had realized that nothing else could help them.

They were amateurs who'd adapted army-acquired know-ledge to the safe-breaking. If they were to be believed and Gideon thought that they were, the idea had been Fitzroy's. But neither of them had raised any strenuous objections and they had come in of their own free will. These were the kind who really worried Gideon most. The old lags, the regulars, the confidence tricksters, the blackmailers, even the dope distributors—all of them were within Gideon's range. He could understand them and he could calculate what they were likely to do. Amateurs were different and their methods were different. They were likely to be more reckless and so more deadly. A man like Fitzroy saw this as a great adven-ture, as well as a chance of making a fortune. A man like Chang saw it as a game to be played with great precision and Chang would never take such risks as Fitzroy, would never shoot his way out. If he killed, it would be cunningly—as he had killed Foster.

Gideon found his lips twisting in a wry, almost bitter smile.

If Lemaitre had said that, he would have jumped on him. It was still a guess. It might not be a wild guess, there might be some reason for making it, but it was still a guess. He didn't *know* that Chang had killed Foster, tried to kill Birdy, was hunting Estelle down. He could not be sure that Foster had not served some other master, too, whom Chang did not know.

That was the trouble; not knowing.

If only he had known at the beginning of the day what he knew now, how much could have been prevented and how much done. If he'd handled Foster differently, Foster might be alive now, and willingly co-operating.

The thought of that hit Gideon with savage force, and suddenly he understood why he had been so easily depressed during the day.

He hadn't liked Foster and that was partly why his temper had broken. With almost any other man at the Yard—the sergeant who'd been so nervous and yet so efficient, for instance—he could have talked reasonably, almost as a friend. He began to go over in his the mind things he should have said to Foster, and the line he should have taken.

His head ached.

He wished Cameron would hurry up with whatever he was doing.

He wondered if they'd catch Fitzroy.

He worried about red-haired Estelle.

He heard the radio telephone buzz, looked at the instrument without enthusiasm, picked it up, and flicked it on:

"Gideon speaking."

"How you doing, George?" This was Lemaitre, speaking direct; and Lemaitre with a lilt in his voice as if his Fifi and his fears were all forgotten. Lemaitre speaking like that was a tonic in itself; cold water in Gideon's face. "Like to meet me over at Shippy's place, Whitechapel?"

"Why, what's on?"

"We've made quite a find," Lemaitre said smugly. "See you there!"

He banged his receiver down.

Gideon fought down the momentary annoyance. In some ways Lemaitre would never grow up, and his attitude now was rather like a boy's. But he was highly pleased with himself and that might mean anything.

Anything.

Gideon was getting up when the telephone rang again, was tempted to go out and ignore it, but conquered temptation.

He had never been more glad.

"Gillick here, G.G.," said Gillick, spitting his words out. "Now I really have got some news for us, trust B2. Eh, old boy? All right, I'll get to the point. We've picked up that chap Fessell you're after, the Islington sweetshop job. One of my chaps thought he saw him earlier in the evening, and kept a look-out. He was in a hotel, dabs make it certain. Shall we keep him here for the night?"

CHAPTER TWENTY

END OF THE DAY

GIDEON drove through the deserted streets of the City towards the East End, munching a ham sandwich which Cameron had laid on. Cameron was looking after everything at the Mid-Union now, and Gideon wasn't needed any more. Gideon wasn't sure that he had ever been needed, but at least he knew all about it.

Depression at the knowledge that Fitzroy was still at large had gone. Fessell's capture was a fresh triumph, and there was the titillating promise of Lemaitre's manner.

Shippy's was a café nearly of ill-repute in the Whitechapel area, not far from the Mile End Road. It was known to be the rendezvous of most of the really bad types in the East End. Murphy used it and most of the men who worked in liaison with Murphy. Many ugly crimes were plotted there. Yet outwardly it was reputable and Shippy, the man who ran it, looked like a citizen *par excellence*. As a café it was not only good, it was spotlessly clean. Shippy, or Luke Shipham, was a thin man who always wore a new white apron, a stiff white collar and a grey tie, whose hair was smartly groomed and brushed to a high quiff. He had never been inside, but had been interviewed a hundred times, and always presented the same bland story and the same bland face: ..

"Nothing wrong happens in my café, Mr. Gideon. I can't refuse to serve men because they might be criminal, can I?"

Most people prophesied that Shippy would slip up one day. Gideon wasn't so sure.

Whitechapel was dimly lit, the wide streets seemed derelict, the unlighted houses were drab, deserted hovels. A few neon advertising signs burned in the High Street, but there was a long gap in them, broken when Gideon came within sight of Shippy's. The name was emblazoned in white neon across the front of the double-fronted café. As Gideon pulled up outside he was impressed, as he had often been, by the smart appearance of the place. Put it in Oxford Street, and it would compare favourably with most restaurants.

A blue sign declared: *"Open Day & Night."*

A squad car was outside, and two uniformed policemen walking up and down. They came closer to see who it was and then touched their helmets.

Gideon felt a quickening sense of excitement as he pushed open the double doors.

The big room with cream-painted walls, blue and red tables and chairs, and the brightly shining urn at the long counter, struck warm. There was a smell of ground coffee. Sandwiches in a glass showcase looked more succulent than those which Gideon had been given by Cameron, and far superior to anything ever supplied by the Yard. A youth stood behind the counter and two plainclothes men of the Flying Squad were sitting at a table, eating and drinking; they jumped up when Gideon appeared.

"All right," Gideon said, "so long as you pay for it. Mr. Lemaitre here?"

One man grinned; the other said: "Yes, sir," and nodded towards the open door leading to the kitchen and the room at the back of the restaurant. Gideon found himself thinking of Chang; and restaurants generally; and the restaurants Chang supplied with tea and other goods.

Shippy, looking correct and aloof, was standing in one corner of the room. A uniformed policeman was watching him. Lemaitre, hat and coat off, sleeves rolled up over those big, swelling arms, sat at a desk with another Yard man, and on a big, deal-topped table there were wads and wads of one-pound notes.

Gideon caught his breath.

"Mr. Gideon, sir," Shippy said quickly. "I didn't know anything about it. A gentleman asked if he could leave his luggage here, and I obligingly said that he could. Mr. Lemaitre is being extremely rude, and——"

Lemaitre looked up, grinning so broadly that Gideon was infected by a kind of gaiety.

"Hark at him," Lemaitre scoffed. "White as blurry snow! Know what we've found, Geo—Superintendent?"

Gideon said slowly and with great, choking relish: "I've got a good idea, Chief Inspector."

"The notes from the Waterloo Station job," said Lemaitre, unable to repress his bubbling elation. "Exactly the same number of packages, and I've counted five, each with five hundred quid in it. Found them in three suitcases." He chuckled. "I'll tell you more when Mr. Shipham isn't with us."

"Mr. Gideon——" Shipham had a walrus-shaped moustache and sad-looking eyes, but they were scared, too, as if he knew that he was really in trouble at last. "I assure you that I knew nothing about it, and I must ask——"

"Just a minute," Gideon said. "Have you made any charge, Chief Inspector?"

"Not yet."

"All right." Gideon was brisk. "You'll have your chance to tell us all about it," he told Shipham. "Now I'm charging you with being in possession of a quantity of treasury notes, knowing them to have been stolen. Anything you say may be taken down and used as evidence. Constable——"

"It's just not right," Shipham protested. "I don't know a thing, Mr. Gideon. In the name of fair play, I appeal to you."

Gideon looked at him coldly.

"Shippy," he said, "in these mail van jobs, three people have been seriously injured, one of them crippled for life. A man was injured at Waterloo this afternoon. That's only one angle. You'll get your chance to say what you like to the magistrate in the morning, and if you want a solicitor, you can send for him. But not until we've got you at the Yard. Constable, ask one of the officers outside to come in, will you?"

"Yes, sir."

"But my business——" began Shippy fearfully.

"You won't be doing any more business to-night, and in the morning your wife can open, if we've finished searching," Gideon declared.

Shipham didn't argue any more.

Lemaitre finished a count and then leaned back, taking cigarettes out of the pocket of the coat hanging on the back of the chair. The other man said:

"Five hundred here, too."

"Oh, it's the same stuff," Lemaitre said emphatically. "Every penny of it, George. What a bit of blurry luck!"

It was almost too good to be true.

"How'd we get it?"

"When we picked up the Snide he was in a bad way," said Lemaitre. "Knocked silly, you know. He said he must get to Shippy's. No one took much notice of it; it's a meeting place for the mob, but it was reported and I noticed it. So I got G5 to keep an eye on Shippy's. Half an hour before I called you on the r.t. another of Murphy's boys came here empty-handed and went out with a case. The G5 chap stopped him. There was a hell of a schemozzle, and three others tried to get the case away. Then Lady Luck looked in, because a squad car was coming along." Lemaitre chuckled and rubbed his hands jubilantly. "Now we've got a busy day to-morrow, George!"

Gideon smiled faintly.

He picked up one of the bundles of notes. Fingerprint men had already been over them, he could see the traces of powder. Prints didn't show up on the edges of a bundle of notes, but a few might have been handled top and bottom. Shippy would probably crack when he knew that they'd be able to send him down. Was it worth trying to work on him now?

Gideon went into a tiny office behind the shop and ran through the papers—bills, invoices, receipts, delivery orders. Then, he began to feel a fresh and tingling excitement; there were several invoices from Chang's restaurant, mostly for tea; yet other big packages marked TEA had a blender's name and address.

Gideon had a funny, choky feeling.

Small packets with a different label were also marked TEA. One was open at the end. Gideon took it off a shelf and looked inside.

There were cigarettes.

He stared blankly—and then began to smile slowly, tensely, unbelievingly. He took out a cigarette, broke it, and sniffed.

These were loaded with marihuana; these were reefers! If he could trace this 'TEA' to Chang——

Gideon laid on a raid before Chang could get warning of Shippy's arrest.

Chang wasn't at the restaurant.

The "tea" was.

Gideon drove home through this dark, quiet London, and the events of the day flitted through his mind. It had been a wonderful day; the day of a lifetime; never to be forgotten.

Chang was under a charge. Mazzioni had been picked up again, and there was a chance of breaking Murphy's power, too, although that would take some time.

Thoughts of the Saparelli family, especially the mother, quietened his jubilation, but the police had done all that anyone could, and time would help, wouldn't it?

He thought of Foster's sister; of Estelle who was no longer in danger. They hadn't got the man who'd stolen Lady Muriel's jewels, a dozen, a hundred crimes had been committed that day which were still unsolved; some would remain so for weeks and some for ever.

They'd have to find Fitzroy, and there was a case all right. Red-handed prisoners, no problem, just routine.

That was how he liked them.

Gideon turned into Harrington Street and saw a light on at the first floor bedroom window of his house. He ran the car into the wooden garage at the corner, and hurried back, suddenly anxious; was one of the youngsters ill?

He let himself in quietly, hurried upstairs, saw a light beneath the door of his room, but nowhere else. So Kate was awake. He called out softly:

"Only me."

He opened the door.

Kate was sitting up in bed with a pink angora wool bed-jacket round her shoulders, a book open in front of her. She looked tired, but her colour was good, and her hair neat in a net he sensed rather than saw.

"What's this?" he asked. "Can't you sleep?"

"Malcolm ran a little temperature," Kate said, "and he hasn't been settled for long. I rang the Yard, and they said you were on your way, so I thought you might like a cup of tea." She glanced at a tray on a bedside table, and the kettle on the bedroom gas-ring. Under a silver dish cover, Gideon was sure, were sandwiches.

Kate hadn't worried to do anything like this for years.

"Nothing I'd like more," he said, and went to light the gas. But she slid out of bed.

"I'll do it. You look tired out. And what's that nasty bruise on your temple?"

"Oh, nothing," said Gideon. "All in the day's work."

He began to undress, and to talk as he did so, only vaguely understanding that it was a long time since he had talked about the day's work with Kate. It was as if the years had been bridged, so that they were together again. He did not think of that in so many words, he just felt that it was good to be home.

THE END